MOUNDNESS

Koosh! Again the gentle sigh of Bucher's silencered Walther. Kroger's weapon went lobbing high into the air and back behind him as he seized himself by the side of the head where the Walther's dum-dum had neatly clipped off his right ear, and launched frenziedly into what could be mistaken for a bloodthirsty warpath dance, screeching, yowling, and baying in rapid succession. Neanderthaloid Rudd forgot his discomfort and stopped to watch, fascinated, until Kroger began to simmer down. Then Rudd addressed Bucher.

"You better kill me, you city-slicker sonofabitch," he snarled savagely. "You better kill me, 'cause if you don't, me'n my brothers'll skin you alive like a bear and turn you loose, and if you're adoubtin' my word, sonofabitch, don't . . . !"

The Butcher Series

The Butcher

#15

Kill Gently,
But Sure
by Stuart Jason

PINNACLE BOOKS • NEW YORK CITY

THE BUTCHER: KILL GENTLY, BUT SURE

Copyright © 1975 by Script Representatives, Inc.

An original Pinnacle Books edition, published for the first time anywhere.

ISBN: 0-523-00671-3

First Printing, July 1975

Printed in Canada

PINNACLE BOOKS, INC.
275 Madison Avenue
New York, N.Y. 10016

KILL GENTLY, BUT SURE

PROLOGUE

The man named The Butcher? The onetime head of organized crime's powerful East Coast Division, then later the dread scourge of the underworld? There is no such man named The Butcher, for "The Butcher," per se, is not a name but a nickname, a title if you please, the bastardization of the name Bucher. And this man named Bucher once did crack the whip over the East Coast Division, then broke with the Syndicate to become a member of an international security organization.

It all began at St. Joseph's Orphanage in Knoxville, Tennessee, years ago on the bleak and wintry morning that St. Joseph's chief custodian, the Reverend Mr. Isham Green, discovered a blanket-wrapped foundling on the orphanage doorstep.

The fact that such discoveries were more or less commonplace at St. Joseph's is not the reason the chief custodian felt neither elation nor depression because of the discovery; even at that early hour of the day the good Reverend Mr. Green was too deep in his cups to feel much of anything, for he truly did love the bottle—providing said bottle contained an alcoholic beverage and was within arm's reach. In all fairness, though, it must be recorded that the bottle was not the chief custodian's only love, for he also loved books. Particularly books dealing with the lives and works of history's great Christian men. These two loves, bottle and books, were contributing factors to the name given the newly discovered foundling, only one word, Bucher.

1

An additional contributing factor was the Welfare Department's commendable practice of giving all orphans destined to become its wards a physical examination as soon as possible. These examinations were, at the time, performed by a young doctor named Allen Adams, a young man who was by nature hysterically ugly and enormously impatient; impatient with life in general and especially impatient with alcoholic orphanage custodians. The examination of this particular foundling took place at St. Joseph's in Reverend Green's two-by-four cramped, untidy office-*cum*-library, the infant lying on a blanket atop the reverend's desk.

There was also atop the desk at that time a volume of short biographies of history's great Christian men, the volume at the time open to the biography of Bucher, sixteenth-century German Protestant and Hebraist. And so it was that when hysterically ugly, vastly impatient Dr. Adams, in filling out a birth certificate, asked: "Name?", the thoroughly intoxicated Reverend Green, eyes on the open book, replied: "Bucher," and Dr. Adams impatiently scrawled "Bucher" in the appropriate blank of the infant's birth certificate. Thus it was that Bucher was named Bucher and nothing else.

The manner in which Bucher became the Syndicate's most feared gunsel, then the dread scourge of the underworld, is an altogether different story, a story that began the day the ten-year-old orphan Bucher climbed into the rear of a tractor-trailer rig loaded with eiderdown bedding destined for the mansion of a jaded millionairess playgirl in Chicago and fell sound asleep. Nor did he awaken when the trailer doors were closed and sealed. The next time Bucher saw the sun was through the polluted air over the Windy City.

In Chicago Bucher survived almost exclusively by the grace of garbage cans until little Luigi Orazio came into his life. After that, things took a decided turn for the better.

Little Luigi Orazio was Bucher's own age, and each

day was brought in a wheelchair by a special nurse to the playground where Bucher had come to hang out. Little Luigi was thin, he was frail, he was emaciated, he was the only son of Tino and Maria Orazio, and he was dying of leukemia.

In that mysterious manner of things only children are given to understand, at first sight Luigi adopted Bucher as his brother. As Mama and Papa Orazio noted the hero worship in their little son's eyes whenever the scrawny half-starved alley urchin named Bucher was around, in their hearts they adopted Bucher too.

Bucher remained in the Orazio household and time passed, and with its passing little Luigi passed on to a better life, and to the grieving parents the presence of Bucher in their home eased somewhat the sorrow of their loss.

Papa Tino Orazio was a man of considerable power and influence in Chicago's underworld in those days, and it was he who first recognized in the young Bucher two exceptionally rare and priceless talents: muscular reflexes so incredibly swift they deceived the very eye, and jungle-animal survival instincts so keenly attuned and constantly alert they bordered on precognition. Due to his own dog-eat-dog background, Tino Orazio saw absolutely nothing amiss in training the young Bucher so that these two rare and precious talents offered the greatest assurance of prolonging the lad's longevity in a kill-quick-or-die environment.

In those post-Capone days, when the ill-famed Four Deuces existed no longer as the throne room of gangland's mighty and the Bloody Bucket existed only in memory, the chiefs of the crime empires that controlled cities across the land decided to consolidate. Thus it was that a nationwide criminal organization known as the Syndicate became a fact of being in the American way of life. Tino Orazio was elected to serve as the Syndicate's first Chairman of the Board.

By this time Bucher was already the toughest, meanest, fastest gun organized crime had ever seen, and due to the underworld's idiosyncratic compulsion for nicknames, was already called The Butcher. On the eleventh anniversary of little Luigi's death a particular incident occurred, the aftermath of which in the eyes of many was proof Bucher's nickname was in no way a misnomer.

Bucher had chauffeured the Orazios to the cemetery that day to place flowers on their son's grave. As they were leaving, both Mama and Papa were machine-gunned to death from a speeding touring car by four torpedoes. Bucher witnessed these brutal murders. He also recognized the killers. The swift and terrible vengeance he wreaked on the four, plus on the others of the upstart underworld faction the four represented, filled nine graves and became legend overnight in the Windy City.

Shortly thereafter Bucher became a young man on the go, a young man whose ice-blood cunning and tiger-savagery called the shots of this incredibly fast and mindless gun who soon blazed his way rung by bloody rung up the corpse-strewn ladder of underworld success until he became the undisputed crime overlord of the Syndicate's East Coast Division.

Then came the day Bucher looked about and asked himself some questions concerning the mean's whereby he had risen to power and obtained a dozen numbered Swiss bank accounts, and when the answers to these questions came back to him he was sickened to the uttermost depths of his very soul. It was at the next business meeting of the Syndicate's crime overlords that he announced he was quitting the organization.

"Whadda ya mean quit?" they had snarled at him in angry alarm. *"You can't quit! Ain't nobody quits the Syndicate and lives! You know that. What's wrong with you all of a sudden, anyway? You gone nuts or something? You got the whole East Coast Division sewed up*

4

tighter'n a drum: the numbers, race tracks, wire services, girlie houses, everything—and you wanna quit? Uh-uh! Quit and how long you think you're gonna live, huh? A day? Two days? A week if you're lucky. Uh-uh, you don't quit the Syndicate! Not never! You're the toughest, meanest son of a bitch we ever seen operate, and you pack the fastest gun since Dillinger came down the highway, but quit the Syndicate and you're dead! Make book on it!"

Yet he had quit anyway; had simply walked off and never gone back. And from that day forward his life became a pressure-cooker existence, at times reminding him of a blood-and-guts Hollywood grade-B extravaganza produced on a shoestring over the weekend. For the day he walked out of the Syndicate his former business associates quietly placed a one-hundred-thousand-dollar dead-only reward on his head. When his trail became so strewn with the bodies of eager-beaver gunsels hoping to collect this reward that interest in it flagged, the Syndicate sparked the interest anew by raising the hit price to a quarter of a million dollars.

Not long after Bucher's break with the Syndicate two neatly dressed young men from Washington located him in a Detroit hotel room.

"Mr. Bucher," said one of the neatly dressed young men. "With your intimate knowledge of organized crime you can be of invaluable service to your country. As a special undercover agent . . ."

They offered him a contract, which he ignored; a salary, which he laughed at, yet in the end he accepted their proposition because in it he saw the opportunity of atoning, in his own mind at least, for some of his grisly past.

Before leaving, the two young men from Washington gave him a telephone number, exclusively his and never unattended, and the code name Iceman. The name of the agency he had agreed to become a part of: White Hat, an organization so super hush-hush no hint of its

5

existence was ever mentioned in the President's fiscal reports or budget requests to Congress.

And thus it was that Bucher, ex-crime overlord of the Syndicate, became Bucher, dread scourge of the underworld.

CHAPTER ONE

Frolicking nude with two equally nude young ladies through the high meadows and the deep gorges of the Great Smoky Mountains was a diversion characteristic of aging satyr and Syndicate mastermind criminal Tony Zubrio, Bucher told himself as he sweated up the steep mountain trail under the heavy backpack. Moreover, it was a diversion with which neither he nor White Hat found fault. But through its Canadian contacts White Hat recently came into possession of information proving Tony Zubrio guilty of a heinous atrocity five years ago. Almost simultaneously with this, White Hat also discovered Zubrio was the key figure in a plot against the government of the United States, a simple plot but with a magnitude sufficient to gravely weaken the nation's internal security.

The atrocity involved the wanton butchery of forty-three Eskimo men, women, and children of the hamlet Iglagook in Canada's Northwest Territories. The plot involved a large number of powerful remote control radio bombs, 1168 of them in fact, which over the past thirty months Tony Zubrio and his men had concealed in public places all across the country; bombs that could be exploded by radio waves from anywhere in the world. And no one except Zubrio himself knew where the bombs were hidden; the ganglord carried with him at all times a small black notebook in which were listed the locations of all 1168.

"And I've got to get my hands on that small black notebook before Zubrio can auction it off to his anti-

American contacts overseas," Bucher muttered to himself. "Then haul Zubrio back to White Hat to answer for the mindless slaughter of the forty-three Eskimos—unless Zubrio wants to play rough and not be hauled back, in which case I burn the sonofabitch on the spot."

But this was of secondary importance and Bucher knew it. First, above all, he must acquire possession of the little black notebook containing the addresses of the hidden bombs. Then, but only then, would he feel free to turn his attention to Zubrio's crime in Canada.

From a pocket of his bush jacket Bucher took a large red bandanna and mopped perspiration from his face—he carried too much gear in the pack. Far too much. Yet he knew nothing of what sort of situation he might encounter here in this wild, scarcely inhabited mountainous region of east Tennessee, and because of this he had brought along White Hat's weapons designers' 9mm reply to the Thompson submachine gun, plus 180 rounds of ammunition in two double-reverse clips. This was extra weight. So was the battery-powered combination standard commercial and shortwave transistor radio receiver, yet he considered it of equal importance to the machine gun—which for lack of a better name the designers had dubbed the Super-Hot. The radio was his contact, in a manner of speaking, with the outside world; beginning tomorrow morning he was to listen at predetermined times to a frequency on the shortwave band to learn if White Hat had uncovered any further valuable information on Tony Zubrio and the bombs.

Bucher stuffed the bandanna back into his pocket and suddenly froze, motionless, listening, eyes raking the foliage on the high side of the trail. Three times since dismissing the taxi on that red clay road at dawn two hours ago, sounds suspiciously like those made by someone keeping abreast of him and parallel to the trail had reached his ears. But now, this fourth time he heard the sounds, he was no longer suspicious. He knew! The sounds were unmistakable. He was being followed! Could Tony Zubrio know of his presence here in the

Smokies so soon? Bucher doubted it. Still, with the crafty and cunning Zubrio the possibility existed, so . . .

Angrily Bucher turned, quickly facing down the trail toward a *new* sound. Someone was above him, someone else on the trail behind. Two of Zubrio's gunsels? Salivating for the Syndicate's quarter-million-dollar dead-only hit price on his head? Then Zubrio *did* know he was in the Smokies.

Silently Bucher shrugged out of the heavy pack, lowering it quietly to the trail and unbuttoning the top of his bush coat to the waist for ready access to the ugly, silencered Walther P-38 in the shoulder rig under his arm.

"Just don't y'all move ary a muscle—sir," an immature masculine voice twenty yards up the trail back of Bucher said. "I got a shotgun centered right square-dab in the middle of your back, so keep alookin' down the trail like y'air."

Futile anger flushed through Bucher. He swore silently in self-disgust. Trapped, by god! Bracketed. The gunsel on the ridge above had rushed forward and descended to the trail ahead of him, and unless his ears lied there was another person on the trail below. Again Bucher swore, angry for letting himself be neatly bracketed by Zubrio's gunsels . . . Yet the person in back of him with the shotgun certainly did not sound like a Zubrio torpedo.

"I done ketched him, Sissy-Glyss!" the immature voice behind Bucher suddenly yelled. "Come on up and see if he's the feller you thunk him to be!"

Bucher watched in silence as from around a bend in the trail forty yards below a young woman in jeans, a man's coarse blue shirt, and heavy leather shoes came into view. The day was already in full and the warm mountain sunshine filtering through the foliage overhead danced in glistening sparkles off the glossy midnight hair gently waving to her shoulders. Her complexion was a deep, rich tan, and as Bucher watched her approach nimbly up the rough trail it came to him that this particu-

9

lar section of the mountains had once been the hunting grounds of the great Cherokee Indian nation. She was still some distance away when she glanced up briefly at him, to which Bucher responded with a nod.

The nod was friendly enough, yet he only permitted the hint of a smile to flicker across his craggy features. The Syndicate-bred survival instincts responsible for saving his life many times now cautioned him that something was aslant, awry, off center, out of plumb—however stated, something was amiss. Though not dangerously amiss, nor deadly, yet amiss nonetheless. Moreover, Bucher was acutely aware, suddenly, of a sense of bafflement. For this reason he confined his initial greeting to a brief nod and the hint of a smile flickering across his face. A second or so later the young woman halted on the trail below him within arm's length.

And, without further warning, Bucher discovered himself to be looking down into the strange yet familiar face of a lovely young woman who looked surprisingly like the beautiful actress, Karen Valentine. Despite this one's rough and somewhat ill-fitting garb she had the same curvaceous, delectable figure and manner of walk; the same enticingly ripe and plump rise of breast and tiny waist; the same flawless, intelligent brow and expressive mouth—with red lips moist and inviting—the same soulful, compassionate eyes and . . . Mentally Bucher staggered, a powerful internal force slugged him low in the gut, and as he searched the depths of her eyes with his own, through his big frame vibrated almost imperceptibly the shock of recognition. Not recognition of her, but recognition that the young mountain woman before him was among the chosen of her sex, one of those women who, in addition to their other disturbing feminine attributes, are also endowed with a rare and precious gift—Bucher knew not what else to call it. Nor had he expected to ever meet another woman so endowed.

Those who concern themselves with such matters claim this gift has been carried by comparatively few of history's famous women. Cleopatra possessed it, they say. And Joan of Navarre and Josephine de Beauharnais. Also Mother Eve. Of the truth of this Bucher did not know. He only knew that once upon a time, years ago, he had encountered this gift, and never since forgotten the girl who possessed it. Nor would he ever.

The gift itself was aught save a delightfully wholesome feminine charisma, but of such special quality and degree that on becoming aware of it individuals of the opposite sex were secretly smitten with enormous pride and joy in their maleness. Possession of the gift was evinced, in part and unknowingly, by the intriguing, provocative way the woman so endowed looked at a man. There was nothing erotic about the look, nothing suggestive, yet it transmitted a subtle and delicate yet earthy and primitive magnetism enveloped in an entrancing aura of intimate camaraderie that triggered an action between a man's body chemistry and his most noble desires which converted him into the particular woman's willing, worshipful slave. And it did more. It gave this willing, worshipful slave the power, and the will, and the courage, to soar figuratively to heights where eagles fear to fly; to walk among the gods and probe the mysteries of the universe; to link hands with the immortals and touch the face of heaven; to understand in full the glory of life and, at least for a while, to know the secret of eternity.

Only by conscious effort was Bucher able to force his thoughts to focus on the unexpected alteration the course of events had abruptly taken. He was about to speak when the young male voice behind him spoke again, a strange, eager yearning in the tone.

"Is it him, Sissy-Glyss? Is he the one you thunk him to be?"

The young woman's eyes, deep gray eyes with gold flecks in them, never wavered from Bucher's face as she nodded, the corners of her ripe mouth tilting upward in a softly radiant smile.

"Yes." Her voice held that throaty timbre which

causes graybeards to yearn wistfully for their youth. "It's him, Goob. Put the shotgun down." She extended a small brown hand, which Bucher accepted automatically, her smile enlarging into a grin of happy excitement, continuing: "Did you ever get the upper hand of those Homerun cigarettes, Sir Badman?"

Slowly Bucher's expression dissolved, fell apart in surprise, and this time he staggered physically, from the kaleidoscope of emotions swirling through his mind feeling not unlike a chicken getting its neck wrung as memory swept him swiftly back through the years to a time shortly before his break with the Syndicate; to a drugstore owned by Lars Johannsen, in Winston-Salem, North Carolina, when he was still crime overlord of the Syndicate's powerful East Coast Division, to a time, in another world, when he had known this lovely young woman standing before him on a trail high up on a ridge deep in the Great Smoky Mountains. Only in those days she had not been the lovely creature she was now; in those days she had been a skinny, scared, starved-looking slip of a girl-child who cashiered at Johannsen's drugstore—a block down the street from the old Elkhorn Hotel, lucrative Syndicate bordello and Bucher's only reason for ever visiting Winston-Salem; except for the times he visited the drugstore with suitcases filled with money for Johannsen to handle for him privately. It was during these visits that, for a reason always a puzzle to him until now, a spontaneous friendship blossomed between himself and the young woman before him now, blossomed quickly and thrived at a time in his life when friends to him were less common than teeth to a marble statue. Her mention now of Homerun cigarettes was in reference to his first attempt at smoking the brand; a pack of which she had sold him. The attempt ended in a fit of coughing that left him gasping for breath.

"No," he said at last, cudgeling his memory almost desperately to recall her name—then he had it! "Homeruns were always too much for me, Jeanie."

From somewhere far down on the ridge below them

came the rusty croak of a purple grackle as Jeanie stared at him in wonder.

"Y-You remember my name?"

"Jeanie Brightfeather. Do you remember mine?"

"You're the only person I've ever known to have only one word for a name." An excited pink crept up over her face. "It was I who nicknamed you Sir Badman."

Bucher laughed, remembering. Back in Winston-Salem she kept insisting no one should have only a single word for a name, and one day at the drugstore had teasingly dubbed him Sir Badman.

"But my name isn't Jeanie Brightfeather anymore; it never was really. I was Jeanie Brightfeather only that time in Winston-Salem. My real name is Pepper Howard. That junior-grade Goliath is my brother Goober."

Bucher turned, facing up the trail, and retreated a quick step at the giant youth lumbering toward him. "My god." Bucher heard himself say the words, though he was not conscious of speaking them.

"He's a whopper, isn't he?" Pepper Howard, moving up beside Bucher, asked good-naturedly.

"Yeah. A whopper."

The object of Bucher's awe loomed eight feet tall, was a yard across the shoulders, and weighed 310 pounds. He wore homemade denim overalls and a blue shirt, his feet were encased in an enormous pair of jackboots, and he carried the Mossberg 500 pump action six-shot repeating shotgun as if it were some weightless plastic toy. As he bore down on Bucher his large, uncomplicated, and open face wore the look of a puppy desperately eager to be friendly. Then Bucher felt his hand seized in a huge paw and arthritic-like pains streaked from hand to shoulder joint as Goober Howard pumped like a man fighting fire.

"Goob, that's enough," Pepper said without heat. "Don't jerk his arm off."

"Duh—Mr. Bucher, sir? Have you really killed 240 men, sir?"

"Goob! Shut up!" The tart acidity in Pepper's tone

13

caused the young giant to drop Bucher's hand at once. "Now pick up Mr. Bucher's pack and get on up the trail."

Meekly, in silence, Goober Howard obeyed, and scant seconds later Bucher saw his heavy pack, held lightly as a feather, disappearing at a gallop around a turn in the trail up ahead.

"Here in these mountains Goob is what they sometimes call 'a mite tetched in the head'," Pepper said quietly. "And as you may already suspect, to him you are the greatest, most fabulous, most incredible hero to walk the face of the earth."

"Me?" Bucher studied her expression to see if he were being ribbed. He was not. "A hero?"

"You're not offended?"

"Flabbergasted is the word. You've told him about me?" Bucher could almost feel her eyes traveling over his face feature at a time.

"Told him about you?" She laughed softly. "I've answered no less than a gillion gillion questions about you since Goob learned I knew you in Winston-Salem. I've also read several dozen articles about you in several dozen magazines several thousand times; Goob has a stack of the magazines yea high. They're in tatters, literally, but they're his most prized possessions. Come on. There's a spring up ahead at a fork in the trail. Goob'll be waiting."

"Just a minute." Bucher took her by the arm as she stepped around him. "You and your brother began following me not long after I left that clay spur road down in the lowlands early this morning. I'd like to know why."

The smile never left her lips as she again studied his face a long moment, finally asking:

"Badman, do you know what section of the mountains you're in? Or the name of the nearest town?"

"I see," he replied thoughtfully. Once before a White Hat case had led him into the Smoky Mountains to a

14

point not far from Sevierville, Tennessee, but close enough to Cosby, Tennessee, to learn that Cosby was the moonshine-whiskey capital of the United States. From where they stood at the moment Cosby was no more than twelve or fifteen miles away straight through the mountains. "Yes, I know the name of the nearest town. I suppose you're in the moonshine business, with a still somewhere around."

"That's right. Goob and I, along with seven other families scattered through the mountains hereabouts. And today was mine and Goob's turn to keep watch on that spur road, that section of it that comes into the mountains. We don't have to bother about the local law. Only the federal tax agents out of Atlanta. There's one named Parsons messing around in these parts now. I thought I recognized you when you left that spur. That's why we followed."

"Because you recognized me?"

"Well—you see—" Pepper turned aside so he could not see her face as she sought an answer, not wanting to tell him wild horses could not have kept her from following once she'd realized who he was. "You see," she started again, turning back. "I'd told Goob who you were, and if I'd made him stay down there on watch he'd never have given me another minute's peace. Come on." She motioned for him to follow. "And please try to have patience with poor Goob, huh? If his questions begin to worry you to death? He doesn't mean anything by them, but to him you're sort of like a god."

Mirth was so little a part of Bucher's life he could almost remember each separate time laughter had come to him, and now, on learning someone might consider such as he a god, even someone a little "teched in the head," he was hard put to restrain himself. Yet he managed—by concentrating on Pepper Howard's figure and the way she walked as she preceded him up the trail. However, the instant he regained complete control of himself he cleared his mind to consider the enigma he

15

had encountered: the enigma of Jeanie Brightfeather who was not Jeanie Brightfeater at all, as she had been as cashier at Lars Johannsen's drugstore in Winston-Salem, but Pepper Howard.

CHAPTER TWO

It did not occur to Bucher that this girl might really be Jeanie Brightfeather, presently using as an alias the name Pepper Howard. It did not occur to him because he would have put his life on the line that her real name was Pepper Howard. Or at least Howard; he had never heard of anyone being named Pepper before, which meant absolutely nothing. She had nicknamed him Sir Badman because she had never heard of anyone having only a one-word name, either. But why, Bucher asked himself silently, if her name was Pepper, did her brother call her Sissy-Glyss? What . . . ?

"I know you're no longer associated with organized crime," Pepper said over her shoulder without stopping. "The Syndicate, Goob's magazines call it. And there'll be folks wanting to know what you're doing here in these mountains so I'm about to ask you. Will I get a lie or the truth?"

"The truth, of course," Bucher lied blandly, ready to pull one of his old chestnuts out of the fire. "Go ahead. Ask."

"Then why?"

"Because I haven't broken all ties with the Syndicate, and won't until I collect the money some of its people owe me. I'm here to find Tony Zubrio." Then he drew the chestnut. "Zubrio is into me for a bundle."

Pepper whirled so quickly she almost sprawled to the trail. "Tony Zubrio?" She frowned in thought. "I know that name. From Goob's magazines."

Bucher was not surprised. Dashing, dapper satyr

Zubrio more than once had caused rumblings of alarm throughout the underworld by his ravenous hunger for the spotlight of publicity.

"Zubrio owes you money, you say?"

Bucher lied gravely. "A mil-seven."

"A mil-seven what?"

"A million and seven hundred thousand dollars?"

"Oh." She started in wide-eyed awe. "He owes you a million and seven hundred thousand real honest-to-goodness dollars?" The way she said it made the sum sound like all the money in the entire world. "Honest?"

Bucher could feel the impact of her eyes on his face, and to avoid them he drew the bandanna from his pocket again and mopped his face, keeping at it until she at last turned slowly and continued along the trail once more.

Before long the trail leveled off for a short distance, then began a gentle decline. A quarter of a mile later they came to a fork: the right prong angled sharply upward toward a gap formed by two tall peaks high above; the left prong continued its gentle downward slope. In the vortex of the *V* formed by the two prongs was a crystal-clear, vigorously bubbling spring of water surrounded by a thick mat of spicy watercress. Goober Howard sat back from the spring at the edge of the cress, beside him the shotgun and Bucher's pack.

"This hyer shore is a fine pack, Mr. Bucher," the young giant rumbled reverently. "A real fine pack."

"Who told you Zubrio was in these mountains?" Pepper asked as Bucher drew a Sierra cup from a side pocket of the pack.

"Syndicate grapevine." Bucher had been expecting the question. "It cost me, but he's here." He rinsed the cup, dipped it full, and handed it to her, waiting till she drank thirstily and returned it before continuing. "The word is that Zubrio and a couple of young lassies have come here to the mountains for a sunbathers' frolic."

"Duh—What's a sunbathers' frolic, Sissy-Glyss?"

Pepper looked Bucher a question. "Isn't that where

they romp around in their—altogether?" When Bucher nodded, and before Goober could ask his sister the obvious, she told him: "In their altogether means they don't wear any clothes, Goob."

"Gor!" the young giant declared to the mountains at large. "That's goin' *nekkid,* hain't?"

"Where do these trails lead?" Bucher asked, dipping himself a cup of water from the spring.

"The left one there," Pepper pointed, "the one descending, leads down into the valley and to our place just this side of the Bloody Foreground. And that right one there that goes up to the gap between those two peaks leads straight to Boogerville, where the three Rudd brothers live."

"Boogerville?" Though Bucher was certain he heard correctly.

"That's what the Rudd brothers call it. And since it belongs to them I guess they've got the right. But it's only a few slab buildings and a few sheds and their still. They live like animals, making whiskey around the clock as long as their runners can get it to Knoxville."

"Hauh!" This from Goober, reminding Bucher of a polite clap of thunder close by. "I'd like to see them godawful Rudds tangle with you, Mr. Bucher sir! By dangies I bet you'd give 'em what for. Wouldn't you, Mr. Bucher, huh? Wouldn't you . . ."

"Goob," Pepper admonished quietly, selecting a spot across the spring from Bucher and sitting down.

"These Rudds sound like real bad actors," Bucher said.

"They de-balled Simon Sipes," the younger Howard blurted. "Took a pocket knife and cut his . . ."

"Goob!" A warning tinted Pepper's tone. "Be quiet."

"But they did, Sissy-Glyss. All three of 'em was in on it. El Dude, Clabber, and Big Snort." He looked at Bucher. "They held Simon Sipes agin' the ground and . . ."

"Shut *up!"*

Goober instantly lapsed into silence, giving his sister a hurt look.

"You're right about the Rudd brothers," Pepper said to Bucher as she busied herself with gathering the largest watercress plants within reach. "As Goob said, there are three of them; Clabber, El Dude, and Big Snort. And Simon Sipes isn't the only person from Bloody Foreground they've caught and made sport with. You see, Bloody Foreground and the region north and east of it is our whiskey-making territory, while Boogerville and the region south and east of it is the Rudds' whiskey-making territory."

"And you don't mix." Bucher put in.

Pepper nodded her dark head. "Right. And never have. And especially not after the Rudd clan—there were seven of them then—after they wiped out the last of the Tiptons." A look of nausea mingled with horror reflected from Pepper's gray eyes. "All thirteen of them."

"Snuck up on 'em in the night, the Rudds did, Mr. Bucher, and butchered 'em like hogs."

"A feud?" Bucher looked from one Howard to the other, wondering if they were putting him on. "I thought feuds went out of fashion with the Martins and somebody."

"I've never heard of the Martins in these mountains feuding with anybody," Pepper told him. "But the Rudds and the Tiptons have been feuding back and forth for as long as anybody can remember. Or had been. Until the Boogerville clan took the Tiptons by surprise that night several years ago."

"What about the law?" Bucher's thoughts were racing ahead, woolling the problem of which direction his action against Zubrio might take now that he'd met Pepper Howard and her huge brother.

"The closest law is in Cosby." Pepper picked the cress up by the stems, submerged them in the spring, moved them gently back and forth several times, then withdrew them and shook free the excess water. "That's the county sheriff. We leave him alone and he leaves us alone. That's the way it's always been here in these mountains and that's the way it is now. I'm not sure I'd want it any other way."

While Pepper was saying this Bucher, to escape a bright shaft of sunlight piercing the overhead canopy and hitting him across the eyes, crawfished backward several feet on heels and elbows, coming to a halt at the edge of the cleared area near a small clump of weeds with finely cut leaves, similar to those of the ordinary carrot, and tiny white flowers half the size of a dime. Some of the flowers were losing their petals, revealing underneath a BB-sized wax-colored berry remarkably like the mistletoe berry. Bucher was about to comment on the carrot-like aspects of the weeds when Goober Howard burst forth excitedly:

"Them! Near the south trail of Bloody Foreground!"

"Them who, Goob?" Pepper looked quickly at her brother.

"Them!" The young giant, in his seated position, made the bouncing, rocking movements of a man on a galloping horse.

"Them *who,* Goober?"

A drumbeat of excitement resounded through Bucher's veins. Since meeting the Howards he'd wondered more than once if he might not have stumbled onto something of value in his search for Tony Zubrio. Yet no emotion showed on his face as Pepper asked a third time:

"Them who, Goob? Who're you talking about?"

"Them!" Leaves on the closer trees quivered. Goober's eyes were now fixed on Bucher and filled with worshipful affection. When Bucher saw the look he felt certain he knew what the boy was talking about. He winked hugely at Goober and nodded in friendly fashion, hoping the gestures would be interpreted as one signifying approval and appreciation. They were.

"Are you talking about the sunbathers, Goober?" Bucher asked in the tone of a man speaking to a close friend.

Goober nodded violently, suddenly in a private glory all his own.

"Where did you see the sunbathers, Goober?" Bucher urged quietly.

"At the Limestone Sinks, on the south trail yond' side of the Bloody Foreground." His voice dropped, abject misery clouded his face. "Only I forgot," he mumbled in utter despair.

"Aw come on, Goob," Bucher coaxed, radiating sympathetic camaraderie, but totally confused by the other's meaning. "Don't let it bother you. It doesn't make any difference."

From across the spring Pepper Howard, pretending to focus attention on the gathered watercress, surreptitiously regarded Bucher with a curious mixture of joy, quiet terror, and infinite tenderness; an instant later she veiled the look to prevent his chance discovery of the aching loneliness, and the fierce yearning, harbored by her heart since first they met in Winston-Salem. It was too soon to . . . If it was not already forever too late for . . .

Goober Howard's massive relief was evinced by his truncated cannon-blast of laughter. "You mean them not bein' nekkid don't make no difference, Mr. Bucher?"

"It certainly doesn't." Bucher's calm attitude in no way depicted the quickened drumbeat of excitement he felt; Goober Howard could only be referring to Tony Zubrio and the two young women the aging mobster had brought with him. "You see, Goob, they'd probably just put their clothes back on when you saw them. Even sunbathers don't go naked all the time. What day was it you saw them?"

The young giant's face went blank. He looked at his sister in helpless confusion, the task of remembering too much for him. Pepper promptly held up one hand, palm toward her and fingers spread.

"Now pay attention, Goob. Perhaps you can remember the day because of something more important happening to you that day." With her other hand she bent

22

the forefinger of the upheld finger toward her. "Was it yesterday?"

Goober shook his head gloomily. "I warn't at Bloody Foreground or Limestone Sinks yesterday."

Recollection blossomed over Pepper's face. "But you were there the day Thunderbird Turner took that Atlanta tax man for a ride, weren't you?"

"*That's* the day!" Goober Howard beamed proudly. "Because I was takin' a tack out of my boot when you told me about the tax man killin' hisself, Sissy-Glyss."

"Last Tuesday," Pepper told Bucher. "Tuesday was the day Thunderbird Turner took one of the Atlanta tax men who killed his kid brother for a ride."

"And bumped him off?" Bucher sounded incredulous; what the hell sort of place was this where thirteen people named Tipton were murdered and no authorities notified? And now this . . . "This Thunderbird Turner killed a federal agent?"

"Oh mercy no." Pepper's soft laughter was captivating. "Thunderbird Turner is one of our runners, one of the men who transport our moonshine from the mountains here to market. Usually Knoxville. Almost always Knoxville. Anyway, Thunderbird's kid brother, Alec Turner, was also a runner until one day three months ago when he was hauling a load and two tax agents chased after him. Their car wasn't fast enough to pass his, but they did manage to pull up behind him close enough to blow out one of his rear tires with a shotgun. You can imagine what happened to Alec; the cars were doing over a hundred on graveled road. Thunderbird swore he'd get both agents, and last Tuesday he got the first one; teased him into a chase with his Special Lady, as he calls it, and when the chase was over, the agent, his name was Cobbs I think, and his car were at the bottom of a deep gorge, the agent dead and his car scattered over a quarter of a mile."

"And that's what Thunderbird Turner means by taking an agent for a ride?" Bucher asked, somewhat fascinated.

"That's right, Badman. Running whiskey is the only crime Thunderbird ever committed. It's not fault of his if a tax agent, or anyone else for that matter, tries to catch him and gets killed running off the road. Thunderbird says he considers a man's life his own personal property, and if the man wants to kill himself it's nobody else's business."

Bucher made no attempt to conceal the sarcasm tinging his words. "And I suppose tax revenue agents from Atlanta make a habit of coming up here in these mountains just to commit suicide?"

"Look at it this way." Pepper could not prevent her smile surfacing into laughter. "Agents come up here from Atlanta and involve themselves with an old, experienced runner, and that's a form of suicide. But it's no affair of the runner's, is it?"

Bucher shook his head curtly. "Moonshining seems like a helluva way to make a living."

"Perhaps it does. To some. But Detroit makes automobiles, Alcoa, Tennessee, makes aluminum. High Point, North Carolina, makes furniture, and here in these mountains we make whiskey. And making moonshine whiskey for a living isn't nearly as terrible as the way some folks elsewhere make their living—including a certain Badman I knew years ago."

Bucher nodded absently, no longer with her. Since their meeting back on the trail less than an hour ago he had repeatedly jogged his memory in effort to recall the incidence of their separation, or the cause of it, back in Winston-Salem years ago, and as she finished talking she suddenly knew. The Syndicate's property in Winston-Salem—a bordello—had burned to the ground late one night. The bordello, the old Elkhorn Hotel, had seemed to burst into flames from ground floor to top all at once, according to the report. No one had escaped. Bucher was not in town at the time, but he had been there that afternoon with Q-Boy Kroger and Sammy Millieto, two of his top torpedoes, to deliver a suitcase of currency to Lars Johannsen, owner of the drugstore where Pepper

24

had cashiered as Jeanie Brightfeather. That was the last time he had ever seen her. Or Johannsen either, for that matter, for soon thereafter came his break with the Syndicate. After that a helluva lot of things had changed. When he returned to the spring, Pepper was saying:

". . . and we didn't make whiskey making illegal; once upon a time you could order a gallon of whiskey from Sears and Roebuck, did you know that? Politicians made moonshining illegal, politicians and some of the big companies who peddle their synthetic slops all over the country. Their little puss-gutted hey-boys known as lobbyists cozied up with certain puss-gutted politicians and first thing anybody knew making your own whiskey was illegal. Our ancestors were making whiskey here in these mountains before there was even a Washington except as maybe a wide place in the road. Or a cow pasture. And as far as our whiskey making and Washington is concerned, Washington can go straight to hell. I'm part Cherokee, not much, but a little—Goob and I had different mothers—and do you know what some of my mother's people are doing right now? Making moonshine whiskey and selling it as alcohol to a big distillery in Frankfort, Kentucky, and their middleman is a federal government Indian agent.

Bucher listened, wondering if she was telling the truth and suspecting she was. After all, even the Syndicate could not exist if the government decided to stop it. He was about to comment on this fact when he found himself looking across the main trunk of the trail over which he and Pepper had recently passed, to a point approximately twenty-five or thirty yards from the vortex of the spring. In an area below the trail, which appeared to be mostly second-growth underbrush, there were some scattered black walnut saplings, several small sassafras trees, a hazelnut thicket, a half-grown sweetgum, and in the center of the hazelnut thicket four of the largest marijuana plants he had ever seen—and he had seen some large ones. The hazelnut bushes themselves were at least eight feet tall, and the marijuana plants, their stalks as thick as Bucher's wrist, thrust eighteen to twenty feet higher. By his expression Bucher gave no sign of his discovery as he brought the topic of conversation back to Zubrio and company.

"Those people you saw at the Limestone Sinks, on the south trail of Bloody Foreground—was it an elderly man and two young women you saw, Goob?"

"Uh-huh." Again the violent nod. "And another man. At first I thought it were one of the Rudds, but it warn't."

"Who was it, Goob?" Pepper asked.

"I ain't never seen him before, Sissy-Glyss. He was— I don't—"

"Were the four people you saw mountain people, Goober?" Bucher asked.

The young giant shook his head, slanting a sidelong look at his sister. "They was all outsiders."

"You should have told me, Goob." Pepper said.

"Aw, Sissy-Glyss, I forgot."

"Don't you forget if you ever see some of that Boogerville tribe at the Sinks or the Foreground. That's our territory. We might wind up like the Tiptons."

"I thought the feud was over," Bucher said.

"For all intents and purposes it is, but who knows what an insane bunch like the Rudds will do? I was kin to the Tiptons, sort of, enough to be called family, a cousin of my mother was one of Eagle Tipton's wives."

"If Tony Zubrio and his friends are in Boogerville," Bucher said, plucking a small stalk of the carrot-like weed from the clump beside him, "then my best bet is to head for Boogerville." Unconsciously almost, as a man will absently put a wheat straw in his mouth, Bucher raised to his lips the carroty weed, his eyes on the spring, when Pepper sprang.

No!

The force of her leap carried her bodily across the bubbly pool of water, and she hit the ground on the other side on her knees, one hand lashing powerfully for

Bucher's face. He was already moving when the sting of the slap cracked against his face.

Bucher swore viciously in alarm at what he had almost done, then thrust the ugly, silencered P-38 back into its holster under his arm. The muzzle of the gun an instant before had been centered between Pepper Howard's soulful gray eyes, which now looked up at him in surprise tinted with disbelief. Quickly Bucher sat down, near enough to Pepper to draw her close.

"I feel like a damn fool," he said honestly. Common sense informed him her unexpected move had not been intended as an attack on him, though his reaction to it had been instinctive, from having survived for years in an uninterrupted, savage battle for survival.

"Did I surprise you?" The question bore tremblly overtones, as if she were too weak to speak stronger. She also made no attempt to change from her snug position at Bucher's side.

"You're full of surprises," he growled good-naturedly though still shaken; only he knew how close he'd come to pulling the trigger. He rubbed the marks on his cheek left by her fingers. "But why?"

"Why did I jump at you?" She pointed to the clump of carrot-like weed, a sprig of which Bucher had been in the act of putting in his mouth when she sprang. "That."

"Yeah?" Bucher looked at the weed in curiosity. "It looks like it might be some sort of wild carrot."

"It is," Pepper said, straightening. "It is a sort of wild carrot—known as hemlock."

"Hemlock? You mean poison?"

She nodded. "Hemlock as in Socrates. It belongs to the carrot family, you know."

"No, I didn't know."

"It kills real gentle, Mr. Bucher," Goober said.

"It what?"

"It kills real gentle."

Bucher opened his mouth in surprise to speak, but instead looked at Pepper for confirmation.

"Goob is right, Badman. I don't know if this is identical to the hemlock Socrates drank, but it's a deadly poison. From what I've been told, after a sip or two of tea made from the plant one just drifts off to sleep and that's it. No pain or anything. Just goes to sleep and never wakes up. We call it Satan's Tea."

"Would that stalk I was about to put in my mouth have killed me?" Bucher asked sternly, a chill trickling up his spine.

"I don't know it would not have killed you." Pepper held him with her eyes as she spoke. "That's the reason I tried to knock it out of your hand. But you moved so quickly I slapped you instead." Impulsively she made him a kiss. "I'm sorry."

"I'm not." Good god! Bucher thought. What a fiendish quirk of fate; after surviving unnumbered kill-quick-or-die nitty-grittys with Syndicate torpedoes over the years, then be put down for the long count by a damn weed. Then, rather lamely as Pepper drew away; "It doesn't look like a poison."

"But it is, Mr. Bucher," Goober Howard rumbled. "Kurt Garfield changed gait and because of it he got so took out with hisself he biled hisself a pot of Satan's Tea and done hisself away with."

Some seconds passed before Bucher managed to untangle and assimilate this—almost. "Changed gait?"

"Yessir." Goober waxed enthusiastic, in glory due to Bucher's attention. "And Kurt was pert' nigh bigger'n them Rudds, too. Then he somehow got hisself double-gaited all the way around. Hair on his face and hands come off, it did, and he begun to talk sorta funny-like. Then one day he biled hisself a mess of Satan's Tea and put hisself outta the way. Some folks around here claim Kurt was a warlock and got hisself tangled up, like, and conjured hisself into a female woman."

Bucher frowned Pepper a question.

Pepper shrugged, nodding. "He changed sex."

"He didn't show any effeminate tendencies? Such as when he was growing up? How old was he?"

"It all happened within a matter of weeks," Pepper said. "And Kurt was thirty-eight."

"You've got to be kidding." Bucher looked thoughtful. The chromosomal shift, or revision, as some authorities called it, which caused a person of one sex to develop the traits, and often numerous physical characteristics, of the opposite sex, was not the mystery it once had been, yet not endocrinology, nor any other branch of medicine insofar as he knew, could pinpoint the cause with absolutely certainty. Nevertheless, this shift seldom, if ever, occurred between full maturity and the climacteric, and thirty-eight would be almost equidistant between the two.

"No I'm not kidding. Goob and I were both at the birthday hoedown last June given Kurt by his wives."

Bucher made no comment on Pepper's use of the word "wives," aware that in this region of the country polygamy was neither a dirty word nor a condemned practice. If one chose to believe hearsay, and in this instance Bucher chose to believe it, the legendary Black Will Walker had, at the time of his death, no fewer than thirty-eight wives. In fact, Bucher never even thought of making a comment on Pepper's words, nor that one of the mountaineers had become effeminate and drunk Satan's Tea to kill himself, for his thoughts were on Tony Zubrio again, Zubrio and the two broads who had accompanied the aging satyr-mobster to the Smokies. He had gone along with White Hat's story that Zubrio's visit to the mountains was only to frolic with a couple of women, yet privately he had not bought the yarn. Not any part of it. There were far too many places better than these mountains to cavort nude, so . . .

"Let's go to the house." Pepper Howard got to her feet. Goober lunged erect, sweeping his pump shotgun and Bucher's heavy ground.

"I'll take the pack, Goober." Bucher extended his hand. "I'm going to Boogerville."

Pepper eyed him calmly. "I once knew you as a man who gave the impression he knew how to take sensible advice. Have you changed to one who now charges in blindly, shooting anything that moves unexpectedly?"

Bucher's lopsided smile acknowledged her reference to his shucking the P-38 instinctively when she knocked the hemlock from his hand. "Okay. What's on your mind?"

"You better come along with Goob and me until I can ask around among our people for information concerning the man you're looking for. I know what I'm talking about, Badman. Those Rudd brothers'll eat you alive and bloody raw."

"Aw Sissy-Glyss now; that ain't so. Is it, Mr. . . . ?"

Pepper shushed him with a gesture as Bucher asked:

"Have you got a phone?"

"Yes, but not for serious business because the Rudds, and maybe sometime the agents from Atlanta, often have a tap on it. For what I've got in mind we don't need a phone. Come on and I'll show you. Goob, you run on ahead and tell Granny we'll have company for dinner."

Bucher shrugged. "Fair enough. I'll appreciate all the help I can get in locating Zurbio." Oddly, he was not at all surprised at Pepper's invitation, though a bit surprised with himself to discover he'd been expecting it. As he fell in behind Pepper a second time, Goober, shotgun, and pack were again disappearing down the trail at a gallop.

CHAPTER THREE

Three-quarters of an hour later they descended the few final steep yards of the ridge into a relatively flat-bottomed valley, and Bucher made no attempt to mask his surprise and admiration when Pepper stopped.

"It looks like a Currier and Ives pastoral," he said.

Pepper laughed softly at his praise. "You know, Badman, once upon a time I read, somewhere, that oxen sweat, men perspire, and young ladies glow, but don't you ever believe it. This young lady put much unadulterated sweat into this place." She swept one hand in front of her, the gesture including everything: the large, single-story house of natural stone half a mile up the valley and the huge barn not far beyond it; the six-foot stone wall at each end of the valley—which was never wider than five hundred yards at any point that Bucher could tell, and bisected through the center by a small stream. The symmetry of each wall was broken near the center in its stretch completely across the valley floor by a heavy gate made of iron pipe, and down the center of the small stream from wall to wall stood a high fence of barbed wire. In the field on the far side of the stream two dozen fat beefs and milk cows grazed in belly-deep fescue and red clover, on the near side was row upon row of vegetables—several acres in Bucher's estimation —and beyond were several more acres constituting an orchard of pear, apple, peach, and plum trees, all of them heavily loaded with fruit.

"If it's nutritious and if it grows in the temperate

31

zone, you'll find it in the garden," Pepper said with understandable pride. "Moreover, it's all organic."

"Remarkable. Amazing." Bucher was honestly impressed by the amount of work that must have gone into the place.

"Oh hush." Pepper, coloring prettily, smacked at him playfully. "Don't lard it on so thick—" She sobered abruptly. "It must be my day for the faux pas, apparently. I didn't realize you were serious. Are you by chance an organic-food advocate?"

"Not especially. I referred to the amount of work put into this place. I can imagine you did sweat a lot." They began following the path at the base of the ridge that led toward the house. "Did you and Goober build the house and barn also? And those stone walls? All by yourselves?"

"Oh no. Our neighbors helped. The menfolk did most of it. People are like that around here if they like you. But Goob and I work the garden and orchard alone. I've got a small tractor."

"I don't see any electric lines."

"That's because you're looking in the wrong direction." She raised an arm, pointing. "There. To the west of the house. If you look carefully you can see the poles leading up the ridge to the west and through that low gap; see?" She lowered her arm when Bucher nodded. "It'd be pretty hard to do all this, the garden and all, without electricity. I've also got a small gasoline-powered electric-power plant at the house for use when the lines are knocked out by storms and such." A dreary sadness crept into her tone. "But I didn't get it done in time to help poor Goob much." When Bucher made no reply she continued. "Goob's particular type of retardation is caused by a protein insufficiency during the first six years of life and insofar as medical science knows, it cannot be corrected. Mentally, poor Goob will always be a child. As for his tunnel vision, the endocrinologist—"

"Come again?"

Pepper spoke over her shoulder without stopping.

"His tunnel vision. Goob can see only directly in front of him, only in the direction his head is turned. This is called tunnel vision and considered to be caused by giantism. You've heard the Bible account of David and Goliath?"

"Who hasn't?"

"An endocrinologic theory is that the giant Goliath suffered from tunnel vision. If David had been armed with nothing but a knife he could probably have darted in and hamstrung Goliath. In order to keep David in sight, the giant was forced to turn round and round like a top."

"Tell me," Bucher said, voicing the puzzler that had cropped up after he discovered that Goob had seen Tony Zubrio and two other persons near the Limestone sinks, and that Goob knew Bucher sought the aging satyr. "How does giantism affect the hearing?"

Happy laughter bubbled from Pepper's ripe lips and she stopped, turning to face him. "I was wondering if you'd noticed that Goob knew you're looking for Zubrio and the two women. How far were we from the spring when you first told me?"

"Fifteen minutes maybe. Perhaps twenty. Or longer. And Goober was already at the spring, waiting."

"Well, at this hour of the day here in the mountains, after the morning feeding of the birds and such is over and everything is almost as quiet as after sunset, the human voice does carry a good ways farther than normal. But Goob would've heard us talking if it'd been in the middle of the feeding hour. And I don't know if giantism is responsible for his remarkable hearing or not. But it is remarkable, isn't it? He claims he can hear a tiny insect crawling on the ground, and not only claims. He can. I've tested him. He can understand what is said at normal human voice level over half a mile away."

"And you call that retarded? 'Teched in the head?' "

"Well," she extended one hand upward, flicking something off Bucher's shoulder. "Perhaps retarded isn't the precise word. Goob is retarded in that his intellectual development will never extend beyond that of the average twelve-year-old. And 'teched' is Old English for 'touched'. The term is used in reference to Goob because of his physical size, perhaps. These mountain people hearabouts tend to equate intelligence with size. They're unable to fully realize or understand how anyone as enormous as Goob has the mind of a child of twelve. Happily, to the simple folk in these hills, it doesn't make one whit of difference." Mirth reflected in her eyes. "Especially to the younger women, and specifically one Sarah Garfield, the late Kurt Garfield's youngest widow. She's eighteen, two years older than Goob, and'd give anything to get her hands on him." Pepper turned, continuing on up the trail.

"And you forbid it?"

"I do *not*." She laughed softly, a delicious sound. "But there are some areas in which Goob hasn't—found himself yet."

"Where did you pick up all this knowledge about giantism, endocrinology, and such? If I can ask without being nosy . . ."

"Oh, I don't consider you at all nosy. My loves taught me; I learned from them."

"Yeah." The word was merely a dry sound.

"They're at the house. With Granny."

"Is that right? I knew polygamy was quite common in these mountains, but yours is the first case of polyandry I've encountered."

Pepper's heritage from Mother Eve instinctively caught the otherwise undetectable note of jealousy in Bucher's tone, the unexpected revelation transforming her wildest dreams into reality so swiftly a strange giddiness seized her, and she might have stumbled and fallen had not the sting of joyous tears in her eyes had a steadying effect. She swallowed hard several times in restraining the new dimensions of her incredible joy, never doubting—though a tiny measure stunned by the swift enormity of the blessing. Never again would she scoff that prayers were never answered.

They were nearing the house and the sound of the happiness in her laughter brought Goober into view from behind it. Over her shoulder she said:

"I speak of books, silly. Those are the loves of my life. I've got gillions, and on just about any subject you can name. If I hadn't learned to appreciate books I might have gone kablooie years ago." She was tempted to stop, to turn and face him again, to let him see in her eyes the reflections of her heart, but decided against it.

"Books?" Bucher demanded in exaggerated disdain, not realizing his tone betrayed the enormous relief he felt but did not immediately understand. "Some lovers."

"Perhaps. But I'd still be just another ignorant hill-billy without them. And believe me, Sir Badman, in these hills there are some dumb ones. Don't misunderstand. I'm not criticizing. I'm stating fact. Being ignorant is one thing. Being complacently ignorant is something else entirely. I read myself to sleep almost every night and have for years, except when I'm at my Secret Place . . ."

"Go on," Bucher told her.

Soft laughter rippled around them. "But if I told you it wouldn't be secret any longer, would it?"

"That's right." Bucher was sure he did not know what they spoke of, and therefore changed the subject. "But I am curious as to how you plan to dig up information about Tony Zubrio without using a phone." Neighbors, as used in this region, not only meant those living close by, but those living closest, which in some cases meant anywhere between ten and twenty-five miles.

"There." Pepper pointed up toward the top of the stone barn.

"I be damn," Bucher muttered in surprise. "Pigeons." On the end of the barn, up near the apex of the tin roof, was the belled landing deck of a carrier-pigeon warren.

"The warren is on the inside, in the loft," Pepper said. "You go wash up while I send a message to start things rolling." She called to her brother. "Goob, show Mr.

Bucher where to wash up." With this she was off and running for the barn, leaving Bucher standing statue-still, as if frozen rigidly in place, cursing in silent self-accusation, bewildered by the perplexity of emotions besetting him. "Your'e going crazy as a bedbug drunk on soured FlyTox," he muttered. "Your head's on crookeder'n hell. You haven't known her much over an hour, discounting the time at Lars Johannsen's drugstore in Winston-Salem . . ." And that, he continued in silence, was a few hundred years ago. Bucher frowned in puzzlement, again recalling the spontaneity of the friendship that had blossomed between them, blossomed and thrived, mysteriously enough, into something that could have become something beautiful . . .

Bucher shook his head roughly, briskly, as a man will when trying to jar his thoughts into line. The girl he knew now as Pepper had, in Winston-Salem, become his friend when he had made a virtual religion of *not* making friends; in those days, when he was still crime overlord of the Syndicate's East Coast Division, friendship could prove to be a fatal thing to have around. Yet . . . Again he shook his head, trying to force into his mind pictures of Pepper Howard struggling helplessly in throes of orgasmic abandonment, but this time the technique failed. It did not cleanse his thoughts of her as it should have done, as it had always done before, with other women who were beginning to occupy too much of his interest, and Bucher frowned deeper than ever, more puzzled than ever—until abruptly into his awareness was thrust the realization that his emotions regarding Pepper Howard were in no way erotically inspired.

Some minutes later, sitting on the screened-in back porch at the rear of the house, Bucher—with a throttle grip on his emotions—watched Pepper race from the barn.

"Golly. I almost forgot," she grinned girlishly, entering. "But all you wanted is to locate Tony Zubrio, isn't it?"

Bucher nodded as they joined Goober, who was already seated at the six-foot-square table massively laden with food.

"Isn't one mil-seven enough reason to want a man?" As usual, Bucher's attempt at lighthearted conversation fell flat, though it took Pepper to make him aware of it.

"Of course. But there are *two women* with Zubrio; your own words, remember?"

After the moment it took this to sink in, Bucher looked at her quickly in surprise. She was busy filling a glass with milk from a pitcher and did not return his look.

"That's all I put in the message anyway," she told him, handing him the filled glass. "Where to find Zubrio."

There was no reason under the sun for him to say it, to tell her the two women traveling with Tony Zubrio were strangers to him, yet he felt an almost vital compulsion to do so.

"That'll be all it takes. I don't know who it is with him. With Zubrio's money, it could be any two of many thousands of women, I suppose. How long before we get action from your pigeon?"

"An hour. Perhaps a little longer. It doesn't take long for the birds to make the rounds. Each of the families of our group raises them, and each family has two of the pigeons raised by each of the other families and wearing that identification mark of the family who raised it. Then each family has its own coded identification mark, so there's never a mix-up either of birds or messages."

"What if Zubrio happens to be at Boogerville?" Bucher asked.

Pepper tossed him a coquette wink. "Does a good general tell the enemy where his spies are located?"

Bucher looked at her in amazement. Pepper Howard was growing more remarkable every minute—a spy right in the heart of Boogerville, right in the center of the enemy camp. But why not a spy in the middle of the enemy camp? Where the hell else should she have a spy if not in the enemy's camp.

see," was all he said, turning his attention to the
ic meal on the table before them.

"In hot weather like this we usually eat a cold mid-
day meal," Pepper explained. "But if you prefer hot
food I can have Granny—"

"No, no." Quickly Bucher shook his head, wondering
where the old woman was at the moment. The vegetables, obviously fresh from the garden, were those that
could be eaten either raw or cooked: green peppers,
tomatoes, carrots, cabbage, lettuce, and the like, along
with soy sprouts, alfalfa sprouts, several kinds of cheese
(including Bucher's favorite, crumb cheese), a twenty-
pound sliced ham, a larger tray of cold, sliced beef, several dozen deviled eggs, a plastic container with almost
two gallons of potato salad, the watercress Pepper had
gathered at the spring—altogether enough food to feed
several dozen hungry field hands. Pepper smiled a small,
secret smile of enjoyment when Bucher saw her watching
his expression as he, in turn, watched the younger Howard load his plate, which actually was a round platter
twenty-eight inches in diameter. And the young giant
was heaping it full with enormous quantities of everything within reach, which with his long arms included
everything on the table. And the glass from which
Goober drank buttermilk was not a glass at all but a six-
quart crock.

"I encourage Goob to eat heartily, Badman," Pepper
said quietly to Bucher, enjoying his fascination. "I—perhaps because it hasn't always been like this for us. And
there are still a lot of families here in these mountains
who wouldn't know a balanced meal if they saw one.
Sarah—I mentioned her to you before. Kurt Garfield's
youngest widow? She was telling me only last week of a
family over on Bone Creek that live mostly on corn.
Cornbread, hominy. . . ."

"Hominy grits?" Bucher cut in.

"What's grits, Mr. Bucher?" Goober Howard asked
around a half-pound bite of cheese.

"Folks in these parts never heard of hominy grits un-

38

til the soldiers returned from the service after World War II," Pepper explained at Bucher's questioning look. "I've never eaten grits, though I read in one of the food magazines I subscribe to that there is some company hawking them nationwide now."

"What about that family on Bone Creek?" It was merely table talk. Bucher wasn't interested in any family on Bone Creek or any other creek he knew of.

"Skinny, scrawny, starving to death, and don't know it. A man, his wife, and several kids gradually dying of malnutrition and ignorance, the worst kind of ignorance, complacent ignorance, thinking themselves well fed because every once in a great while the diet includes a few squirrels or maybe a groundhog or a rabbit or two, but starving nevertheless. As I almost was the first time I ever saw you at Lars Johannsen's drugstore in Winston-Salem."

"That wasn't the time I bought the Homeruns, was it? The first time we met, I mean. I've forgotten."

"The twelfth."

"The twelfth?"

Pepper Howard sat rigid as stone staring at Bucher, a deep crimson creeping slowly up over her throat to darken the deep tan of her face. Instead of having the appearance of being uttered voluntarily, her next words seemed to escape reluctantly in a dry, wooden whisper. Even so, there was a brave defiance to the whisper.

"You bought the Homeruns the twelfth time you and your men came into Johannsen's drugstore."

Bucher nodded, blankly looking at the forgotten food in his plate. Q-Boy Kroger and Sammy Millieto had been his two best gunsels at the time, good with a roscoe but without enough smarts to mastermind a double cross, for it was not at all uncommon for him to carry staggering sums of currency into the drugstore in those days, most of which he usually left with Lars Johannsen, who was also on his payroll. But his private payroll. Not the Syndicate's. Johannsen had connections in Europe with which he had constructed a beautiful pipeline to

39

syphon currency into Bucher's numbered Swiss bank accounts. As a matter of fact Bucher had turned over the last bundle of cash to Lars Johannsen for shipment overseas the same night the old Elkhorn Hotel had burned to the ground. Bucher had never seen the man after that night, yet Johannsen had started the money through the pipeline, for it had shown up later on a deposit slip. And not long after that night, only a matter of days if he recalled correctly, he had walked out on the Syndicate. The night the old Elkhorn burned was also the last time he'd ever seen Johannsen's underfed cashier who called herself Jeanie Brightfeather.

And this same girl, who now called herself Pepper Howard, remembered after all these years that it had been exactly his twelfth visit to the drugstore that she had sold him a package of Homerun cigarettes. There was only one reason a woman would remember such an incredibly insignificant event as a man purchasing a package of cigarettes so long ago, and that was because of the man himself . . . A knowledge which had been hovering in the back of Bucher's mind came forward without invitation, and he knew, or rather he acknowledged to himself what he had known for some seconds.

Absently, aimlessly, he maneuvered the tines of his fork about between crumb cheese and potato salad, embarrassed over Pepper's embarrassment at his discovery that she once harbored a strong case of puppy love for him, for the moment not suspecting he erred on two counts. The emotion Pepper had harbored for him in Winston-Salem had never been that passing fanciful affection known as puppy love, but that vigilant, tenacious, and enduring love with which singularly few men have ever been blessed. This was the first point on which Bucher erred.

The second was his hasty assumption her affection had faded with time. It had not—a fact Bucher discovered the instant he raised his eyes to meet hers—and the knowledge of his discovery, plus additional knowledge he discovered in her soulful eyes set him atremble

40

inside in the manner of the martyr burning at the stake who suddenly sees angels descending to his rescue. Earlier, during their first few moments after meeting back up on the trail, Bucher had detected about her a certain mysterious quality he had known in but one other woman in his life, a charismatic femininity, delightfully wholesome, which somehow projected a commingling of subtle and dainty yet earthy and primitive female magnetism enveloped in an aura of intimate yet delicate camaraderie. Since first becoming aware of its existence years ago, and in small part for lack of a better name but mostly because so few women possessed it, he had always thought of this mysterious quality as "the gift," for such was precisely what he had once assumed it to be. Now, as he sat looking across the table into Pepper's gold-flecked gray eyes, he abruptly realized how thoroughly mistaken his assumption had always been. It stunned him. For the space of a half a dozen heartbeats he lost control of his senses and they swirled crazily hither and yon before settling back in place. For the second time within two hours the powerful internal force slugged him low in the gut. For a millisecond insane laughter crackled through his brain. Then he seized control of himself once more. Almost.

"D-do you know—?" No less than a dozen different times since meeting on the trail he had been about to voice the question, but each time it had somehow gotten sidetracked. Even now other words shoved themselves forward. "I bought the Homeruns the twelfth time I was in the drugstore?"

"So now you know my secret." Her small chin lifted perkily in defiance. "So boo, Badman."

Silently Bucher loosed a pent-up breath, voice normal when he spoke. "Strange, but life plays funny tricks. The same night the old Elkhorn burned; that afternoon I bought the Homeruns, I was the luckiest man in the world and didn't even know it."

A tomb-like stillness settled over Pepper. She spoke in a little-girl voice. "You really believe that?"

41

"Not in Winston-Salem. I believe it now."

"You have new eyes, as we say in Cherokee."

Being fluent in three Iroquoian dialects, one of which was the Cherokee, he knew the expression she referred to, but only nodded. Then: "I was blind in those days, blind as a bat; blind as a stupid bat. A stupid, idiot bat." The words carried an undertone of quiet viciousness.

No warning foretold the blossoming of mindless terror in Pepper's breast from momentarily mistaking the meaning of this strange man she had loved with an aching, torturous love so long and so hopelessly. She dropped her gaze. The misunderstanding vanished. So did the terror. Joy wild and fierce surged in to replace it. And Pepper's reaction to this swift reversal of violent emotions was a noticeable quivering of her lower lip as she raised her eyes again to meet his, asking as calmly as she was able:

"About Jeanie Brightfeather?"

"About many things. Not long after that I walked out on the Syndicate, you know."

"Yes. I know, though I didn't until some time after that." Then she said what she knew her conscience would make her tell sooner or later. "My husband told me."

A peculiar lightheadedness smote Bucher. "Your husband?" It had not occurred to him she might be married.

She nodded, sensing his distress, saying quickly to dispell it. "He died the same week the Elkhorn Hotel burned."

"I didn't even know you were married."

Pepper inhaled a shaky breath and plunged on. "He liked Goob; I had Goober with me in Winston-Salem. The man I married was extremely fond of Goob. He was dying of emphysema. Progressive emphysema it's usually called; sometimes galloping emphysema because it acts so fast. Anyway, he was rich, my husband was, and wanted to leave Goob some money but said it wasn't possible because of his family unless we were married. So I married him for his money one morning in Winston-

Salem within minutes after the marriage license bureau at the courthouse opened; his lawyer arranged for a waiver of the waiting period. He died that night. And Goob got the money."

"That was the only reason you married him? The money?" Bucher was not certain why he asked this.

She sat straight in her seat and leaned slightly toward him, holding him with her eyes, holding gently but firmly so he did not get away. "That's what I had to keep telling myself else I never could have gone through with it. Get the money for Goob, get the money for Goob, I kept repeating over and over while the judge married us. But if you'd looked at me twice there in that grubby drugstore, Badman, or even given some slight indication you knew I was around, that I existed, I suspect I'd have passed that money up. But as it turned out it wasn't so bad. A bride and a widow in the same day. Wow, did I ever have a case for you." A warm smile overspread her face and she kicked him lightly under the table. "Better hide some victuals, Badman. There may be work for you to do when the pigeon returns."

Bucher was glad the course of their conversation changed. He wanted to keep it from the past, their past at least, if he could. "Is your Granny not eating?"

At that instant the kitchen door opened and the person Pepper and Goober called Granny emerged onto the porch, a water glass full of amber liquid in one hand, a corncob pipe in the other. Her hair, waist length and snow white, lay in two thick plaits, one on either side of her breasts. Bucher had seen her when food was being placed on the table earlier, and knew by her complexion and bright little obsidian eyes she was full Cherokee, though as yet he had not heard her speak. Now, as she passed the three of them at the table she nodded politely but said nothing, continuing past the table to a hickory splint-bottom rocker near the end of the porch, which was bathed in warm sunlight. She sat the glass of amber liquid on a two-by-four stud divider in the screened wall

43

beside the rocking chair, then sat down, puffing on the corncob pipe.

"Granny rarely eats more than two tiny meals a day," Pepper said. "One at sunup and one at sundown."

Bucher studied the old woman from the corner of his eye. She was scarcely four feet tall, could weigh no more than eighty or eighty-five pounds, and despite the warm weather wore a dress of solid black closed at the throat and both wrists, the hem reaching to within an inch of the floor. Over this she wore a black-and-white-checked gingham Mother Hubbard apron, held about her tiny waist by ties in back. The apron also reached to within an inch of the floor.

"She is Cherokee?" Bucher asked.

"Yes. Pure Cherokee. She speaks no English except a sort of hodgepodge English-Cherokee by which she and Goob communicate."

Bucher hesitated, but saw no reason for keeping his knowledge of the Cherokee language secret from the three on the porch with him. He ran the fluid syllables silently through his mind to make certain he had them correct, and was about to speak to the old woman when Goober paused long enough during his vast intake of fuel to say:

"Go ahead, Mr. Bucher sir, speak to Granny in Cherokee."

Pepper gave her brother a somewhat startled double take of surprise as Bucher turned toward the end of the porch and said quietly and with great respect in Cherokee:

"Will you not take food with us, Old Mother?"

At first Bucher thought she had not heard, or perhaps had misunderstood, then she turned her head slowly, looking at Goober and smiling as if to say that now she believed his affirmation that the big stranger spoke her language. Bucher saw a sparkle of pleasure in her obsidian eyes when she looked at him, her laughter an ancient but happy cackle.

"No, not at this hour," she said in reedy tones, addressing Bucher by the non-translatable term *Kayalan,* its closest English equivalent "warrior who performs with courage and valor." "But if you are here at sundown, Kayalan, we will share food together."

Bucher was not unaware of the distinction showed him by her implied invitation, for in spite of lying history books and the lying, stupid hacks who wrote them, the ancient Cherokee social order was not only matriarchal in concept but in practice, down to even the materfamilias of each separate family unit. Thus, an invitation to dine with a tribal matriarch was indeed an honor.

"For now I sip my whiskey and smoke my pipe," the old woman continued. Then to a somewhat flabbergasted Pepper: "Perhaps Kayalan would like a glass of whiskey, child. Offer him a drink."

Pepper's ripe mouth moved, though without sound until she managed vaguely: "There's whiskey . . ."

Bucher shook his head, but his reply was to Granny. "Thank you, Old Mother, but I seldom drink when there is work to be done. Perhaps if I am here at sunset I will take a glass."

The old woman nodded politely, concluding the conversation, and began rocking gently, puffing on her corncob pipe and from time to time sipping from the glass.

"Granny wants me to take her over for a few days' visit with Dolly Fancher this afternoon," Goober rumbled to his dismayed sister.

"Who told *you* Mr. Bucher spoke Cherokee?" she demanded in exasperation.

"Why Sissy-Glyss, one of them magazines of mine says Mr. Bucher speaks nineteen different languages." He looked at Bucher in unfeigned pride, as if Bucher's knowledge was his own prized possession. "Don't you, Mr. Bucher?"

Pepper stared at Bucher in nonbelief. "Do you?" she demanded accusingly.

Not without considerable effort did Bucher restrain

his laughter. "I'm afraid the magazine was mistaken, Goober."

Goober started in surprised, instant agony to discover his idol was of dross with clay feet; a low moan of despair escaped him and he cringed under Pepper's triumphant look of reproach.

"Counting dialects I speak twenty-one," Bucher continued quietly; the silence following was thick enough to cut.

"Twe-twenty-one? C-counting dialects?" Pepper ventured timidly.

Goober snorted in ecstasy—his god did *not* have clay feet! The non-ceilinged sheet-tin roof of the porch became a metal diaphragm amplifying his thunderous salvos of laughter. In the kitchen a metal cooking utensil jarred by the reverberations clanged to the floor, and from various points about the house windowpanes rattled threateningly.

"Oh Goob!" Pepper burst forth, ending abruptly with a polite, almost prim: "Hush." Struggling with mirth, she cast an oblique glance at Bucher, lost the struggle, and smothered a rush of giggles with both hands.

"Anything wrong?" Bucher teased when she quieted, enjoying her merriment.

"I . . . oh . . . no, silly!" She funny-faced him. "I'm happy. Okay, Badman? Now eat."

Bucher was no longer hungry though he pretended to eat out of courtesy, an amenity Pepper ignored altogether, and several minutes of relative silence ticked past until Bucher remembered yet again the question so far repeatedly forgotten. But not this time. He thrust a forefinger in Pepper's direction.

"Do you know who you look like?"

Pepper, rapt in a gossamer pink world of daydreams, was taken by surprise. "W-what?"

"Do you know who you look like? Look exactly like?"

"Karen Valentine. The actress."

46

"You know?"

"Of course I know, Badman. Since I first saw her on television." Her question bore no hint of feigned innocence. "Do you think Karen Valentine is pretty, Badman?"

"I do, though not merely pretty. Beautiful is better but trite. Stunning is better still. So is breathtaking. It's a shame on the language one must go hackneyed and cliché-ic to describe a woman of her rare loveliness of face and form." Bucher stopped, not wanting to beg the point, but the breathless happiness wreathing Pepper's countenance and the softly radiant joy in her large gray eyes prompted him to continue. "Karen Valentine without doubt is the ultimate in charm and poise, and as for looks, Venus de Milo, Aphrodite, Cleopatra, Jean Harlow, and Marilyn Monroe are too vapid and colorless to be compared with her. She is exquisite, ravishing, and endowed with a dainty perfection of feminine grace that declares her the ultimate embodiment of all things desirable in a woman; she is God's incomparable creative achievement placed on earth as a priceless blessing to all lovers of beauty everywhere."

Only the sounds of Goober's vigorous mastication troubled the thick silence following until Pepper's soulful sigh of dreamy ecstasy joined them. Bucher pretended renewed interest in the food, anxious she did not misconstrue his excessive verbage insincere servile flattery, for in rerunning the words swiftly through his mind he acknowledged with something akin to mild but exhilarating shock that in spite of their gooey sophomoric flavor he meant every syllable. But to her, Pepper Howard. Not to Karen Valentine.

As if reading Bucher's mind, the dreamy quality in Pepper's eyes at that instant segued into a puzzled question.

"Wow and double-wow, Sir Badman. The way you lay it on makes hillbilly me feel like a goddess, but—" She studied his face closely, wondering. It was clear she

47

did not for a second doubt his description referred to her and no one else.

"But what?" Bucher asked.

"Well . . ." Her laugh was a bit shaky. "But nothing, I suppose. I—was a bit curious as to how you thought of me, and when you said I looked like Karen Valentine I thought—well—you know." She exhaled heavily. "Anyhow, I asked and I got told. Nobody can deny that."

"I wasn't speaking of Karen Valentine."

"I know you weren't, Badman. I sort of now wish you had been, though." She poked the pink tip of a saucy tongue at him, attempting to fend off the uncomfortable depression trying to envelope her. "But if I should ever ask again, don't jet off on a tangent, huh? Hew a little closer to the line."

This was the cue Bucher wanted. "You mean lie?"

"No, darn it, I mean tell the truth." The tinge of haughty defiance in her expression, Bucher knew, was a defense mechanism.

"I didn't lie. I wasn't talking about Karen Valentine and I didn't lie. And your thinking I did doesn't make it so."

When his meaning registered Pepper Howard, literally, stared openmouthed in surprise. "Oh," she said at last in a tiny voice. "Oh. Oh." Then she jumped to her feet and fled inside.

"You hafta kinda overlook her sometimes, Mr. Bucher," Goober Howard offered philosophically. "Her bein' a female woman and like that." He shoveled a pint of potato salad into his mouth, tamped it down with several small tomatoes, then hoisted the six-quart crock of buttermilk and glug-glugged contentedly.

"Something's been puzzling me, Goob," Bucher said, hoping Pepper would return soon.

"What's that, Mr. Bucher sir?"

"Why do you call Pepper Sissy-Glyss?"

Confusion overspread the young giant's face, and he looked about quickly in various directions in search of Pepper. She obliged them both by emerging from the

48

kitchen doorway. She made a happy grimace at Bucher, sighing resignedly.

"Come on, Badman." She held out a hand. "It had to come sometime, so let's get it over with and behind us. Come on. Follow me."

Bucher followed her through a door located behind where Goober sat at the table into a small, sparsely furnished room: a thick pallet on the floor against the back wall, a low stool, a pitcher and water basin, and little else.

"This is Granny's," Pepper said over her shoulder in passing through the room to a door beyond. "This is exactly what she wants and won't have it any other way. I once suggested a TV set and she was horrified at the idea."

The door across the room opened into a long hallway, which informed Bucher his assumption the house was small was mistaken.

"This is a helluva way to locate Tony Zubrio." Bucher commented absently, entering the dim coolness of the hallway behind her.

"Ooh, don't be so impatient, Badman. Wait till the pigeon returns. Look." She motioned with her hands, indicating both walls of the hallway. "The lovers I told you about; part of them. And my bedroom has a thousand or so more."

Bucher's eyes, quick to readjust to the dimmer light of the hall, saw that bookshelves lined the walls from ceiling to floor, shelves filled to capacity with every category of book in English; or such was Bucher's impression as they moved swiftly past, emerging into a huge room paneled on three sides by glass jalousies. It was another bedroom, though there was nothing about the decor to suggest it belonged to a woman. In fact, to Bucher it looked very much like a well-equipped library into which a bed had been placed.

"This is my bedroom," Pepper said. "And these are what I brought you here to see. And laugh, or faint, or cry out in fear or whatever you like. I'm used to it."

49

She pointed to the wall of the bedroom immediately beside the door on their left, where Bucher saw the bust-photo of a woman in an oval frame. There was something strikingly familiar about the face in the picture, only he could not find a connection with it in his memory at the moment—until Pepper said:

"She was my sister. One of them. But those certificates on either side of the picture are what I brought you to see. They're enlarged birth certificates; Goob's and mine." She pointed to the one on the left. "That's Goob's. And this, right here, is Goob's real name."

Following her fingers with his eyes Bucher stared, wondering if this was a gag of some sort. "That's— Goober's real name?"

"That's it," Pepper said with unshakable finality. "Sears and Roebuck Howard. His mother named him from a catalogue. My name came from a patent medicine bottle." Again she pointed and again Bucher's eyes followed her finger. "Go ahead and laugh, Badman, if you want. If I ran across somebody with Glycerin Hygroscopic Trihydroxy for a name I'd laugh too. Come on." She took his hand. "Let's go into the kitchen and get you a glass of whiskey anyway, or you might not get your work done after all."

They returned to the kitchen in silence, and Pepper poured him a small glass of whiskey before either spoke. It was Pepper who broke the silence.

"Aren't you going to laugh?" She set his drink on the kitchen table, and instead of reaching for it, Bucher reached for her, drew her close, and found her lips for his.

"Gol*ly*," she marveled softly when their lips parted. "My name has never affected anyone like that before, but since it does: Glycerin Hygroscopic Trihydroxy." She offered her lips to him again. And several minutes passed before either of them bothered with words again.

"I don't understand why our names didn't throw you, Badman," she at last whispered against his mouth. "Names like Glycerin Hygroscopic Trihydroxy and

Sears and Roebuck are enough to give some folks hysterical seizures."

"Laughter?"

"Mostly."

"I don't think they're comical. Not really. Perhaps I've got a thing between my ears about names since mine has only a single word. I suppose you could say I represent one extreme and you the other; I know now why Goober calls you Sissy-Glyss. How come your parents hung such an unusual handle as Glycerin Hygroscopic Trihydroxy on a defenseless infant?"

"Badman, I was the last of seventeen children; Goob and I had different mothers—but I told you, didn't I?—the last of seventeen children born to incredibly ignorant, incredibly superstitious parents. To the best of my knowledge I am the only one who can read and write. As far as I know all the others are dead; they left the mountains soon as they were old enough and just never came back and I don't blame them. My mother was Cherokee-Irish, and after seventeen children, in addition to the back-breaking toil and the deprivations of life in general here in these mountains, she simply lost the will to live. When the midwife wanted to know what my name on the birth certificate was to be, my poor mother pointed to the words 'glycerine hygroscopic trihydroxy' on a medicine bottle on a stand beside the bed, then turned her face to the wall and died. And that's the way I got the name I have. The midwife, hardly less ignorant than my mother, simply copied the words from the bottle to my birth certificate. And that's why Goob calls me—"

"Sissy-Glyss?" Alarm colored Goober Howard's rumble from the porch. "Somebody is acomin' from Boogerville way, Sissy-Glyss."

CHAPTER FOUR

Goober's alarm was instantly reflected in Pepper's gray eyes. She stepped free of Bucher's embrace, lifted a pair of binoculars from where they hung by their strap on a peg beside the kitchen's rear door, and hurried out onto the screened back porch. Bucher followed, going directly to his pack leaning against the wall behind Granny's chair, danger-warning hackles astir on the back of his neck.

"There, Sissy-Glyss." Goober, who had risen to stand beside his sister. "They's two of 'em. See? Yon side of the barn."

Pepper fitted the binoculars to her eyes as Bucher adjusted the small, compact 30-power telescope, the distant side of the mountain showing above the roof of the barn leaping swiftly at his eyes as he dialed through the telescope's opaque blur. In a second he picked up movement of two male figures, in dress similar to that worn by Pepper and Goober. Gently Bucher focused the glass. The two newcomers were no more than a mile away, and at that distance his 30-power glass should show him the whites of their eyes.

One of the men carried a rifle, and to judge by their manner in creeping through the underbrush coming down the side of the ridge, it seemed to Bucher they were obviously intending to put the barn between them and the house in order to approach the house undetected.

"They've come through the Bloody Foreground but didn't give the signal." Pepper lowered her glasses and looked at Bucher. "All of our people know about the

Bloody Foreground signal; it's a stick of dynamite with cap and fuse. Anyone coming this way through the mountains places the dynamite on a stump and lights the fuse. Noise of the blast tells us to expect visitors. Those two coming now are from Boogerville."

"One of them may be from Boogerville," Bucher told her, the glass to his eye and watching with meticulous care. "But the other isn't." The other was Q-Boy Kroger. According to underworld scuttlebutt Kroger was now the Syndicate's number-one torpedo on the west coast, a cold-blooded Syndicate executioner who killed dispassionately, mechanically. But once upon a time, when Bucher still rodded the organization's East Coast Division, Q-Boy Kroger had been one of his fastest guns.

"Kayalan." From her rocker Granny spoke quietly to Bucher in Cherokee. "Those who approach are enemies. Do not let them harm my children. The girl and boy are all I have left in this world."

"Have no fear, Old Mother," Bucher replied in the same language. "The two are but gadflies who I will swat with one hand."

"You want to take that back before it gets cold and you can't, Badman?" Pepper asked. "One of those men is Clabber Rudd, and nobody swats one of the Rudd brothers like he's a gadfly. He's killed half a dozen men, or more, with his bare hands."

Bucher did not answer, but instead returned to his pack, stowed the telescope, and from the main compartment of the pack drew a sturdy black plastic case three by six by eighteen inches, opened it, and sixty seconds later had White Hat's latest experimental weapon assembled. Experimental though it was, in Bucher's opinion it was little more than a 9mm version of the old Thompson submachine gun, which was saying quite a bit for the gun at that. Even so, due to the science and techniques of metallurgy this 9mm, labeled the Super-Hot, was over four pounds lighter than the old Thompson, had far greater range, and instead of the old fifty-round drums used two forty-five-round reversible clips.

"Pepper." Bucher's tone brooked no argument, and she reached his side as he snapped the clip in place. "This is the way you operate this gun." He explained thoroughly but with a minimum of words. "The safety works like this. When you get ready to fire, push the safety off, aim the muzzle in the general direction, and pull the trigger. The gun will do the rest to anything within a thousand yards. Now here." He yanked the bolt back then let it slam forward, jacking a shell into the chamber and arming the piece. "It's ready to fire when you flip the safety off and pull the trigger."

She accepted the machine gun with huge eyes, a pallor beginning to show beneath her tan. "B-but where are you going?"

"I intend to be a reception committee of one when those two bums reach the barn. If anything goes wrong, if I goof, this Super-Hot is to protect you and Goober and Granny." To Granny he said: "Do not worry, Old Mother. I have much experience in dealing with varmints and things that crawl from under rocks." The old woman cackled in delight as he left the porch and hurried to the big stone barn, careful to keep the barn between him and the two men approaching from the far side.

The barn, though of stone, was in all other respects like the log barns common to this part of the country. Stalls for animals were on each side of the wide runway, and above them were the areas used for the storage of winter feed. Separating the stables on the left was a narrow tackroom, from the walls of which hung various kinds of harness, rope, several yard-long strings of fiery hot red peppers—used in conjunction with turpentine in the two-quart bottles on the floor against the wall below. As the regionally accepted medicine for farm animals—a coil of quarter-inch hemp line, and even a worn saddle. Though Bucher had not seen any horses in the field below the house, near the end of the tackroom stood a farrier's stand and a small, portable bellows. The bellows was near the door at the opposite end of the tackroom. This door was open and Bucher hastened to it on cat's feet, the sound of male voices reaching his ears as he stopped barely inside it.

Peeking around the edge of the door facing Bucher saw Q-Boy Kroger—lean, hard, purposeful in his movements —and a man almost as big as Goober Howard walking hurriedly toward the door where Bucher stood, though still seventy-five yards distant. Between the newcomers and the barn stood a couple of rough carpenter's horses made of two-by-fours, a pile of second-grade pine lumber, a stack of three-foot stakes, and a sledgehammer, as though someone intended building a pigpen of sorts. These things Bucher fixed in his memory through habit, to prevent him from stumbling over any of it if a nitty-gritty broke loose and he had to move fast. And Bucher did not doubt there would be a nitty-gritty if Q-Boy Kroger got half a chance. The bastard liked to kill. The pair were within fifty yards of the barn when Bucher stepped through the tackroom door into the open.

"The Butcher!"

Q-Boy Kroger stopped in his tracks, staring hard in surprise. His companion did likewise.

"You boys lost something in this neck of the woods?" Bucher asked quietly.

"What the hell are you doing here?" Kroger demanded angrily. He wore overalls, blue shirt, old felt hat, and boots —the same as Clabber Rudd—but even from that distance Bucher could smell the powerful French cologne Kroger had imported especially for his use. The sweetish lilac-lavender odor of the stuff reminded Bucher of a Middle East cathouse.

"You're keeping strange company these days, Q-Boy," Bucher said, ignoring the question. "You had better taste when you worked for me." Then Bucher tried a shot in the dark. "Tony Zubrio'll get you killed."

Kroger started violently in surprise. "Why?" He attempted a snarl but couldn't quite pull it off. But this in no wise misled Bucher; in his own particular line of work, Q-Boy Kroger was as good as they came.

"Because I'm here to kill Tony Zubrio," Bucher told

55

the other, wondering at Kroger's surprise when Zubrio's name was mentioned. "Get in the way and you'll get the same. Or if you want to settle it now, go for that cut-down Iver Johnsen .44 Magnum under your arm."

Kroger's right shoulder twitched spastically as he almost involuntarily went for his gun. An unwholesome liver-hued tongue slithered forth from under his nose and slurped wetly around over his lips.

The large man beside Kroger, Clabber Rudd, looked uncommonly like a gorilla that had lost a good deal of its hair on the lower part of the face. This Neanderthaloid aspect was enhanced by the man's posture, for he stood with legs slightly bowed and bent forward at the hips; the low brow that slanted rearward, the massive forward-thrusting jaw, and the tiny, animal-alert eyes that bored into Bucher without wavering all combined to suggest that Clabber Rudd in some respects was not long out of the Stone Age. In one huge paw he carried a Marlin 10-shot .44 Magnum lever action rifle, an ideal brush gun. When standing erect the man could not be much shorter than Goober Howard. Yet simply looking at the man Bucher knew Clabber Rudd was one great helluva lot meaner than Goober Howard could ever be.

"My frind here ast you a question, sonofabitch," Rudd snarled, and unlike Q-Boy, brought it off, for snarling with him was a natural form of expression. When he spoke he revealed a mouth full of teeth, yellow and blocky except for the two incisors below and above which protruded above the others like fangs. When Bucher did not reply at once, he spoke again, snarling more viciously than before. "You gonna answer my question, stranger, or do I tear it outta your gullet with my bare hands?"

"You're in my territory, punk," Bucher said easily.

"Yore territory?" Rudd blinked his beady little pink eyes suspiciously. "This hyar's Howard territory!"

"Not anymore." Bucher added on the spur of the moment. "Now it's mine by right of marriage." He paused; Kroger and Rudd seemed dumbfounded, then explained solicitously. "Pepper Howard is my fourth wife."

"Yore a l'ar!" Murderous, furnace-heat rage crackled through Rudd's declaration. "I'm hyar to pleasure me some with that sassy-assed Pepper Howard and . . . !" He swung the rifle around.

Koosh!

The ugly, silencered Walther P-38 that appeared in Bucher's hand before Rudd's rifle moved an inch sighed softly, its 138-grain dum-dum slug slamming into the receiver housing of the Marlin. Clabber Rudd leapt high and screeched in blind rage, dropping his piece and wringing one hand with the other to massage feeling back into it.

This time Q-Boy Kroger did not catch the involuntary twitch, but plucked his cut-down Iver Johnsen .44 Magnum from under his arm, an evil gloating on his unwholesome face.

Koosh!

Again the gentle sigh of Bucher's silencered Walther. Kroger's weapon went lobbing high into the air and back behind him as he seized himself by the side of the head where the Walther's dum-dum had neatly clipped off his right ear, and launched frenziedly into what could be mistaken for a bloodthirsty warpath dance, screeching, yowling, and baying in rapid succession. Neanderthaloid Rudd forgot his discomfort and stopped to watch, fascinated, until Kroger began to simmer down. Then he addressed Bucher.

"You better kill me, you city-slicker sonofabitch," he snarled savagely. "You better kill me, 'cause if you don't me'n my brothers'll skin you out alive like a bear and turn you loose, and if you're adoubtin' my word, sonofabitch, ast her. Or that simple-headed eejit with her."

"It's Goob and me, Bucher," Pepper said from behind him. "We came to see if we might help."

For no other reason than the hell of it, Bucher bowed graciously to the two men. "Gentlemen," he intoned with royal grandiloquence, "my wife, Mrs. Pepper Howard Bucher. Mrs. Bucher, I caught these two varmints sneaking up on the place. By the way, Pepper, what number wife are you? Fourth? Fifth? Sixth? With so many it gets confusing after a while."

Despite the gravity of the situation Pepper colored prettily in happiness. "My number doesn't matter, dear, as long as we're married and I have you to protect this territory."

"He ain't gonna protect nothin'!" Clabber Rudd glowered threateningly. "Not after me and my brothers finishes with him, he ain't." He looked at Bucher. "And since you got yourself married to this sassy-assed—"

"You got a big mouth, punk," Bucher said.

An almost fiendish joy overspread Rudd's Neanderthaloid features. "Mayhap you'd like to close it for me, city slicker." Without giving Bucher time to answer he had waddled forward half a dozen apish steps when a tiny metallic click from Pepper's direction was followed by a jarring burst of staccato-thunder from the Super-Hot in her hands, pulverizing the ground scant inches in front of Clabber Rudd. He jerked to a stop, gawking at Pepper.

"Throw aside that .38 from under your overall bib, Clabber Rudd." Her voice was quiet. Deadly quiet. "And do it with only two fingers. One tiny false move and I cut you in half."

Rudd obeyed in a frenzy, flinging the .38 far to the right, still gawking at Pepper as if unable to believe what he saw.

"The Butcher carries a switchblade," Q-Boy Kroger hissed from behind Rudd.

Bucher put the Walther on "safe" and handed it to Goober, plucked the switchblade from its sheath above his left ankle, and gave that to him also.

"Keep a close eye on Kroger," Bucher told Pepper, "while I teach bigmouth a lesson about how to respect another man's wife."

Rudd still stared at Pepper in bafflement; apparently, Bucher assumed, because the man's hillbilly intellect refused to consider a woman capable of independent thought and action outside the bedroom or the kitchen.

"Uh-uh." Rudd shook his head lugubriously, meaning

the set-to with Bucher was off. " 'Cause when I begin teachin' you our kind of mountain manners, city slicker, that new 'wife' of yorn'll cut me in two anyway." He made "wife" sound like a revolting obscenity.

"Don't interfere." Bucher glanced at Pepper as he told her this, at the same time dropping his hands into the side pockets of his bush coat, lacing the fingers of each through the brass knucks it found there. "If bigmouth takes me, let him go. Only protect yourself, Goober, and Granny. Is that clear?"

"Bucher please," she pleaded in a tremulous whisper. "Don't do it, please. He'll kill you."

"Bucher yet she calls me," he chided. "Have you no faith in Badman?"

Rudd and Kroger watched intently, missing nothing, and at Bucher's first move forward, the gorilla-like Rudd moved forward also, with alacrity and zest, his pink little eyes aglow with bloodlust—and foolishly, overconfidently, plunged headlong into what a matter of seconds convinced him was the path of two invisible sledgehammers powered by thunder and triggered by lightning.

At Rudd's forward lunge Bucher knew his assessment of the man's fighting technique was accurate; the man depended on bulk and brute strength to overcome an opponent. This was made obvious when Rudd came in with head slightly lowered, not unlike a charging bull, but with hairy paws extended to the fore in the manner of a wrestler seeking to grapple. It never occurred to Bucher to hassle with this mountain Hercules on Rudd's rough and tumble terms, for this would give Rudd the edge and to do this contradicted every survival instinct the Syndicate had bred into Bucher. Moreover, Bucher fought only to win, and to win as speedily as possible. Therefore, when Rudd charged with hairy paws extended Bucher's hands came out of his coat pockets, each hand curled into a fist and each fist armored with murderous brass knucks. He clubbed the hairy paws aside and struck without mercy; with pitiless savagery.

One-*crunch!* Two-*crunch!* Three-*crunch!* Four-*crunch!*

The knucks sledgehammered their deadly warcry into Rudd's Neanderthaloid face with disastrous results: they broke his nose, ripped away an entire eyebrow plus a large, thick pad of flesh, mangled his mouth, and shelled his teeth like corn. Stunned, almost as much by unbelief as by his injuries, Clabber Rudd from Boogerville swayed on his bowed legs until clear vision returned to his undamaged eye—whereupon he made the same mistake again. And again came the swiftly repeated four-times-*crunch!* But this time he did not stand weaving on bowed legs waiting for his vision to clear. He flopped to the ground with a gutsy "Oooooff!" and lay motionless.

"Merciful heavens." Pepper's tone held nothing if not unfeigned amazement.

"Well Sissy-Glyss, what'd you expect? You thunk Clabber Rudd'd whup Mr. Bucher?" The young giant was scandalized. *"Mr. Bucher?"* His tone accused her of sulfuric blasphemy.

"Oh, Goob, all right." Her quiet laughter was trembly with relief. "Scoot over. I'll kneel and worship beside you." When she moved to stand beside Bucher her eyes still reflected incredulity. "Did you—? Is it—that—still alive?" With a movement of one foot she indicated the inert Rudd.

A small geyser of crimson fog plumed upward from Rudd's smashed nose each time he exhaled, and even as Pepper asked if he were alive the man made gobbling noises and commenced trying to sit erect.

Bucher accepted the Walther from Goober and stashed it beneath his arm, saying to the youngster as he did so: "Take the switchblade to the tackroom and bring back four lengths of stout cord to tie these bums up with." As Goober lumbered off to obey Bucher said quietly to Pepper: "Do you know if our friend here speaks Granny's language?"

"I'm not positive, but I'll bet he doesn't. Why?"

Bucher replied in Cherokee. "You return to the house. I intend to put the fear into these two cruds."

"Is one permitted to ask by what means?" Pepper asked in the same language.

"One is," Bucher grinned. "I'm going to convince them they're about to get the same treatment the Rudd brothers gave—what's his name? Simon Sipes? Any—"

"Oh mercy no!"

"Of course not. Only they're not to know otherwise until they're too terrified to venture back to this neck of the woods again. And in doing so I might have to use language unfit for maidenly ears—maidenly in spite of a certain book on your bed when you were showing me your and Goober's birth certificates." Brought out by one of New York's most prestigious publishing houses, and written by an internationally famous husband-and-wife team of doctors after a decade of research, the book Bucher saw dealt with the physiology and techniques of ideal marriage and, according to advertising blurbs describing it, in polite but unmistakable terms the book left nothing whatsoever to the imagination. "So you scoot on inside."

Pepper frowned in perplexity, trying to remember the book he referred to, the frown quickly vanishing when she did.

"You—devil!" she laughed, nodding toward the battered Neanderthal at their feet. "Would you rather I learned from a thing like that?"

"Here's Goober with the cord—take their pistol and that rifle with you. I'll follow in a bit."

After she was gone with the guns Bucher turned to Q-Boy Kroger who, despite his missing ear, now stood with arms straight up. The man appeared terrified.

"Where's Zubrio?" Bucher spat at him.

Kroger gulped rustily. "I—I don't know, Butchy. Honest to god I don't know."

"What are you doing in Boogerville?"

"I came to buy pot. Bugsy Moline sent me."

"Frisco?"

Kroger gulped again, nodding. "These ignorant hillbillies have got ten million dollars worth of the stuff and don't even know it."

"How long you been with Moline?"

"Well—I don't know, Butchy. How long's it been since you walked out on the Syndicate?"

"Who sent you to the west coast?"

"Tony Zubrio. He was a big man in those days, and still is, I guess. But not nearly as big as he used to be."

"Keep talking."

"He cooked up some kind of deal with a guy named De Jourst, in France. Did it against orders from the top. Been working on the deal for better than two years now."

"What sort of deal?"

"Nobody knows. That's what the Syndicate brass are hot about. Word is that Zubrio has been warned he'll either straighten up or else, and I don't have to tell you what the 'else' means."

"What are you and that apey-looking bastard sitting there doing over here?"

A noticeable tremor of terror coursed through Q-Boy Kroger's frame. "Butchy, I swear to god—I didn't know the young lady was your wife. On my sainted mother's holy name I didn't know it—"

"Then you and Rudd *did* come over here to molest her."

Kroger bleated wanely, shivering again. He knew the code. The Butcher might forego revenge for a simple, straight-out attempt to collect the Syndicate's quarter-million-dollar dead-only hit price on his head, but for molesting The Butcher's woman, or even being caught in the act of intending to molest her, Q-Boy Kroger knew full well he need expect no mercy.

"*Butchy!*" he screamed thinly. "I didn't know *why* we were coming over here! *I didn't know!* He just said 'Let's go over to the Howard place.' He didn't say anything about making her put out to him!"

"Okay, I'm going to give you a chance. For old time's sake . . ."

"Yeah-yeah-yeah!" Kroger's outburst of relief seemed premature to Bucher, yet he said nothing. "Yeah-yeah, we did get along good in the old days, didn't we Butchy, huh, didn't we Butchy?"

"If you're in these mountains tomorrow I'll know of it, Q-Boy," Bucher told the other coldly. "Then I come after you, but not for an ear. I take your scalp. Understand? Now get the hell out of here while I castrate this gorilla-looking sonofabitch."

Q-Boy Kroger was fleeing like a man on fire by the time Bucher finished speaking. To Bucher it seemed the farther he went the faster he got. Never had he seen a human being cover ground on foot so fast.

Bucher's apparent sudden change of heart was not without purpose, though he was not sure precisely what that purpose was. Even so, there was something about Kroger and Rudd's appearance here that had a peculiar ring to it, yet he was unable to pinpoint why. For the time being he filed the notion in back of his mind. Right now he had business with ape-boy, who was just managing to return to full consciousness.

"Over there," Bucher snarled, pointing to one of the carpenter's horses he'd noticed earlier. "Drape your carcass over one or I'll put a bullet between your eyes."

Clabber glared with his one good eye and wanted to resist but the eye betrayed his fear. He was convinced Bucher meant exactly what he said. Therefore he did as he was told, and minutes later Goober had the man tied securely across one of the carpenter's horses, bent across it from the waist, a wrist tied to an ankle, then the ankles tied together. The man was helpless as a bulldogged steer.

"Now what, Mr. Bucher sir?" Sears and Roebuck "Goober" Howard asked when he finished. Goober had just seen his earthly deity perform exactly according to his expectations in the matter of the clobbering Rudd had received because of it was in a tidy little heavenly cocoon of his own.

"Goober, what was it the Rudd brothers did to Simon Sipes?"

"They de-balled him. Held him against the ground like

63

he was a bore hog and cut out his seeds with a pocket knife, they did."

Bucher, in possession of his switchblade once more, kept stropping the long, slender blade back and forth on his open palm the way a barber strops a razor, making certain he stood in full view of Rudd's upside-down view between his spraddled legs. Rudd commenced to whimper spasmodically in the manner of a wounded animal waiting for certain death. After some seconds of this the Neanderthal gave way completely and collapsed inside, his reason deserting, and began to howl in mindless terror.

"Goober," Bucher said in a loud voice between howls. "My knife is pretty dull and I don't want to butcher Rudd unnecessarily when I trim him. Have you got a knife?"

"Yessir, only it ain't much of a knife. Not for nothin'." He drew from an overall pocket an ancient Barlow which was no longer really a knife but the remains of a knife, its single blade broken off to within a quarter of an inch of the handles. "Like I said, Mr. Bucher sir," the young giant opined somewhat philosophically, "It ain't much of a knife on account of they ain't much of it left."

"Then I'll have to sharpen mine. Is there a whetstone in the barn?"

"Uh-uh, but they's one in the kitchen. Sissy-Glyss got a humdinger where she keeps the knives and forks and things."

Bucher could not have come up with a better idea had he labored over it. Rudd had just about reached the point of seldom return and Bucher saw no gain rendering the man insane with fear. Surreptitiously he motioned for Goober to follow him to the tack room.

"Now listen carefully, Goob," Bucher said in low tones when they entered the tackroom. "I'm not going to trim Rudd. My knife isn't dull." He extended the blade to one of the strings of fiery red peppers hanging from the wall, flicked his wrist and one of the hard, tough pods split from stem to tip, sending a tiny shower of small seeds down onto the quart bottles of turpentine on the floor below. "I only pretended we were about to operate on Rudd to frighten the man enough to keep him away from here."

"Then we ain't gonna de-ball 'im then, Mr. Bucher?"

"Goober, if we did a terrible thing like that we'd be no better than the Rudds, would we?"

Retarded or not, the young giant was deeply impressed by this simple logic. "Boy, I sure wouldn't like to be as low-down as them Rudds, Mr. Bucher."

"Good. Now here's what we'll do. You stick around out here for a while, fifteen, twenty minutes or so, then you tell Rudd real secret-like that you don't approve of what I'm going to do, so while I'm still in the house sharpening my knife, you say you're going to turn him loose if he'll make a run for it, because if he doesn't run I might catch him, bring him back, and operate on him anyway. Can you do it?"

"You want me to actual turn Clabber Rudd loose, Mr. Bucher sir? Honest-like?"

"That's it exactly. Honest-like. Can you do it?"

"Why—'course Mr. Bucher. Ain't nothin' to it. I'll let 'im go directly. Only that howlin' and screechin' comin' from a Rudd do sound purtty, Mr. Bucher. Awright if I hear it for a while longer?"

"Why not?" Bucher grinned; if Goober Howard was a wee mite "tetched in the head" he still had a lot more smarts between the ears than many people Bucher had known.

Addressing the world at large with a vociferous complexity of terms ranging from simpering prayer to blistering oaths, the helpless Clabber Rudd had a one-man hullabaloo going full blast as Bucher left the barn for the house, the sounds seeming to increase in volume as they progressed. But Bucher forgot them at the sight of Pepper Howard. Her lovely face glowed from a wondrous inner radiance he found enchanting.

"Where's Granny?" he asked on noting the old woman's absence.

"Inside resting. Goob is taking her across the mountain later this afternoon to visit Dolly Fancher, a friend of Granny's for almost a hundred years. She has absolute faith Kayalan can take care of any difficulty that arises. Do you always inspire trust and faith in people?"

Bucher jerked a thumb toward the barn. "Would you say those sounds Rudd is making are inspired by trust and faith?"

"Oh, silly. You know what I mean—let me rephrase it. Do you always inspire either trust or terror?"

"I've never given the matter any thought." He frowned in reflection. Now that he did give the matter thought, albeit briefly, it came to him he'd met few people who regarded him with an absence of emotion, who had felt neither strongly affirmative nor strongly negative toward him. "Why? Is that bad?"

"Certainly not. I'm just a bit surprised at how readily Granny accepted you. That isn't at all customary with her."

"Pepper, are you sure Goober is retarded?"

She looked at him quickly with a curious mixture of emotions. "Why do you ask?"

"Because he doesn't act the way I've always supposed a retarded person acts."

"I only know the poor child's mental development has been arrested." A dull agony underlay her words. "It is extremely difficult for him to learn completely new things, yet what he manages to absorb he retains. For instance: I don't remember having read in any of his pseudo-crime magazines about you speaking nineteen languages—" she stopped, listening. Rudd's caterwaulings, oddly, took on new dimensions of fear and pain.

"I told Goober we were not going to give Rudd the Simon Sipes treatment. Will he obey?"

"Wild horses couldn't make him do otherwise, since *you* told him. I saw the other one fleeing. What was his name?"

"Q-Boy Kroger."

"You let him go?"

"He won't be back to bother you again. I made him a promise, and if he does come back he knows damn well I'll keep it."

Bucher went to where his pack leaned against the wall and was disassembling the Super-Hot to return it to its carrying case when Pepper, a strangled quality in her voice, blurted:

"Badman?"

Quickly Bucher looked toward her. "What is it?"

"That man! Q-Boy Kroger. I kept thinking I'd seen him somewhere before but couldn't recall where or when —if not a photograph of him in one of Goob's magazines . . . but . . . but, *he* was one of your men in Winston-Salem! Each time you came to Johannsen's drugstore he and another man were with you. Even the last time you were there. The night the old Elkhorn Hotel burned."

"You're exactly right," Bucher said, wondering if this was what kept nagging at the back of his memory, for something most definitely was. Or had been until now. He snapped shut the Super-Hot case and stowed the weapon back in his pack, rising to his feet. "Q-Boy Kroger and Sammy Millieto. In those days they were my bodyguards." His voice dropped, as if addressing himself. "Tony Zubrio isn't in Boogerville. Kroger was too scared to lie—unless he's changed one helluva lot since the old days. But supposing the creep *was* lying . . . ?"

"I heard him mention marijuana?"

"Do the Rudds hustle pot?"

"They'll hustle almost anything for money, and heaven knows there's scads of pot growing all through these mountains. There's a story, and I believe it, that three years ago a wealthy hippie got hold of several hundred pounds of marijuana seed and scattered them from a light plane all through these mountains."

Bucher nodded. He had heard the same story, with

slight variations now and then, no less than a dozen times in the past few years. "When we were up at the spring I saw four plants nearly thirty feet high, the highest I've ever seen."

"I'm not surprised." Pepper shrugged indifferently. "I've got no use for the stuff. I've tried it by smoking, in brownies, mixed with spaghetti sauce, and quite frankly I don't like the effect it has. It's too much like relinquishing control of my mind to something else. You say the plants were thirty feet high? I once heard it's only supposed to flourish in hot, dry climate, but that's all hooey. Devil's Tea, or Satan's Tea, or whatever one chooses to call it, according to a leading horticulture magazine, isn't even a native of the Western Hemisphere, but it grows like ninety all over. You don't like relinquishing control of your mind to anything else either, do you?"

"How did you know?"

"Granny told me you and I are *ethawaha*."

Bucher was not familiar with the meaning of the Cherokee word. "What does it mean?"

Pepper smiled mysteriously, shaking her glossy black hair. "But I might tell you later. If you're a good boy. Granny—"

The verbal agitation beyond the barn abruptly swirled upward, amplified into horrendous torrents of savage, searing agony counterbalanced by equally savage, maniacal screeches of fear, and Goober hove into view from behind a corner of the barn, clutching himself about the middle in helpless mirth, his dynamite-blasts of laughter startling birds into flight a mile in all directions from the house and barn area. From the other end of the barn Clabber Rudd burst violently upon the scene but quickly left it in the general direction by which he and Q-Boy Kroger had approached earlier, though without the barn directly between him and those watching from the house. Unbelievable as it was at first sight, Rudd covered ground at a far swifter speed than had his cohort Kroger, yet his flight was repeatedly interrupted by what ap-

68

peared to be some powerful unseen force. He would dash forward a dozen yards or so, then in mid-air would curl into a tight knot and cannonball to the ground, howling, screaming, and gobbling insanely. After flip-flopping about a bit clawing and beating and chewing at the ground in a frenzy of madman desperation he would again shoot into the air, streak blindly forward again, and within another dozen yards or so hurl himself to the ground once more for a repeat of his unusual conduct.

The sight had Bucher and Pepper thoroughly baffled. But Goober sagged weakly against the side of the barn still shouting with laughter, tears streaming down his face as he watched Clabber Rudd continue his mysterious cavortings. Very soon the man passed from sight into the timber far up toward the head of the valley.

"Goob, what on earth?" Pepper asked her enormous brother when he came to the house.

"Why," Goober said proudly. "I turpentined him. I turpentined Clabber Rudd."

"Oh, Goob." Pepper turned quickly and disappeared into the kitchen, shoulders shaking with mirth.

"They was some turpentine out yonder in the tack room," Goobre continued to Bucher. "Well, I turpentined 'im real good, Mr. Bucher sir, and for good measure added some pods of that hot pepper in the tack room too. I bet he don't stop runnin' till sundown a week from tomorrow."

Bucher gave himself over to the good feelings and leaned against a porch upright, laughing without reservation.

"Hit was awright for me to turpentine 'im, wasn't it Mr. Bucher?"

"Perfectly all right, Goob, and when word spreads through these mountains you turpentined Clabber Rudd you'll be the most famous hero since Daniel Boone."

"Looky yonder!" Goober pointed to a spot above the near apex of the barn roof, and Bucher saw a carrier pigeon come fluttering down to light on the small landing platform. A thin line Bucher had not noticed before, between the top of the barn and the porch, moved a tiny fraction, and almost directly above his head, attached to the porch roof, a small bell tinkled merrily. By then Goober was on his way to the barn.

Pepper emerged from the kitchen and stood waiting beside Bucher; Goober came lumbering back toward the house three or four minutes later. A hush settled over the trio as Pepper pulled apart the tiny plastic capsule Goober handed her, then carefully unrolled the thin cylinder of tough paper she took from inside it. Bucher was unable to decipher the message, which was obviously in some kind of code, but Pepper read it readily enough.

"Tony Zubrio and three other people, two of them female, are at the Limestone Sinks," she said. "Near Bloody Foreground."

Bucher turned toward his pack. "I've got a map . . ."

"Forget it, Badman." She touched his arm. "I'll show you where the Sinks are." She walked to the edge of the porch and checked the angle of the sun through the screen. "But we'll have to hurry. Goob, Granny'll be awake soon. You take her over to Dolly Francher's and stay there. Understand?"

"Aw, Sissy-Glyss—"

"Goober!"

"Oh, awright, Sissy-Glyss. I'll stay with Granny." But he was miserable, crestfallen.

"Goob," Pepper said affectionately. "After what you did to Clabber Rudd today there's no telling what that Boogerville gang will do. You stay with Granny until I send for you." She went into the kitchen again, returning almost instantly with a small slip of the carrier-pigeon message paper. "Right now I'm going to send for help. From anyone of our group to come stay here till we get back from the Sinks."

"Zubrio may no longer be at the Sinks," Bucher said. "Does the place have any sort of accommodations or conveniences?"

"A stone hut. And it's an ideal place to run about in your altogether."

"Can you include in your message what Goober did to Clabber Rudd?"

Pepper smothered soft laughter as she sat down at the table, cleared by Granny while the three of them were at the barn. "Oh yes. I can put what Goober did to Clabber Rudd in the message. And when Sarah Garfield hears of it she'll come charging over here to protect her hero from one and all other similar female hero worshipers hereabouts."

"Why, Sissy-Glyss?" Goober's obvious innocence caused Bucher to look Pepper a question, which she answered by a negative shake of her head, and devoted her attention to the message, encapsulated a minute later and given to the young giant to send.

"When Granny wakes up tell her I've gone to the Sinks with Mr. Bucher. Do you understand?"

Goober nodded and left, affording Bucher the opportunity of asking: "Does Sarah Garfield want to marry Goober?"

"I'm not sure that makes any difference to Sarah." She sighed heavily. "Poor Goob. This is the only time I've never been able to help him. And I can't. How on earth would I tell him? If I were his brother it would be altogether different, but—and—he just doesn't know *anything*. Does Badman have any advice?"

"Sure," Bucher replied promptly. "Forget it. That's one thing no one has to be taught. Or one of the things, I should say. Eating is another; an infant doesn't need to be trained to eat. Or sleep. Or eliminate waste. And the youth of the species don't need to be instructed on how to carry on the sex act. When Sarah Garfield gets to Goober, she'll show him what to do. But if you want me to talk to him, I will." He hoisted the heavy pack from the floor to his back and shrugged into the harness. "Come on. Let's move it."

CHAPTER FIVE

Three grueling hours and, Bucher was positive, no less than a gallon of perspiration later, where they were or the distance they had traveled since leaving the house he did not know. He was oddly content to follow while Pepper led, the seldom-distinguishable trail always angling up, or around, or both, twice skirting the lower edge of high meadows where dun-colored deer placidly grazed. Not long after they passed through the second meadow Pepper turned right, still following no visible trail, and led the way down the ridge at a sharp angle. The meadow was still in sight when they entered a deep gorge choked by a thick stand of Ponderosa pines. At this new direction blessed relief flushed warmly through Bucher's aching thigh muscles. Soon the welcome sounds of a rushing stream drifted up to them from far below, the volume of the sounds increasing in proportion to their descent, indicating to Bucher they were headed for the bottom of the gorge. Some minutes later they emerged abruptly from the relative darkness of the heavy timber into the bright sunlight of a small, tight clearing, perhaps three-quarters of an acre in size, a third of which was occupied by a crystal-clear pool beneath a fifty-foot waterfall pouring over the lip of a limestone cliff that formed the upper extremity of the clearing.

"This is the Limestone Sinks?" Bucher asked.

Mysteriously Pepper shook her head and touched a finger to her lips for silence, a strangely eager little smile teasing the corners of her ripe mouth. She motioned for

Bucher to follow and, still without speaking, walked at the water's edge around the left side of the pool until they reached the base of the limestone cliff. Here Pepper moved confidently out from the bank at an angle that would take them directly under the falls, walking on a narrow shelf an inch below the surface of the water. Bucher followed, though somewhat more cautiously because of the heavy pack he carried, marveling that the shelf they walked on was virtually invisible except when looking at it straight down. Pepper approached the edge of the falls, and Bucher kept his eyes on the shelf as he inched along behind. When he glanced up briefly to get a general picture of their bearings, he froze in place. Pepper was gone! Disappeared!

Aw hell! Bucher said to himself in disgust. Because of the pressure-cooker he lived in he had long since grown accustomed to expecting the worst. Pepper couldn't disappear. Not with him within three or four feet of her. He moved forward aggressively toward the edge of the falls to investigate and was under the falls, near the center of the spill, when a small brown hand took him by the arm.

"In here, Badman," Pepper smiled eagerly, tugging his arm. Not a little puzzled, Bucher obeyed, stepping off the shelf and out of the water, then through a large vertical fissure directly behind the falling water and in the face of the cliff. Two steps later he was in an enormous, pleasantly cool limestone chamber, save for an earthen bottom. The chamber was roughly in the shape of a giant inverted teacup, the ceiling twelve feet overhead, the floor forty feet from one side of the chamber to the other.

At the rear of the chamber sat a large box made of plywood. A dozen feet to the left of the box, directly under another fissure leading into the dimness overhead, was a crude fireplace made of clay, lime, and stones. Beside the fireplace, which was fitted with a heavy wire grill, lay a large heap of firewood, an axe, a one-man crosscut saw, and a hatchet. There were numerous sharpened stakes driven into mud seams at points along the wall, and from two of these hung white gas lanterns. Bucher noted all these details once, then again to fix them in his mind, before turning to the young woman beside him. Pepper Howard seemed on the verge of bursting with pride and joy—and a certain anxious eagerness.

"What is it?" Bucher finally asked, surprised that the sound of the water falling so near did not interfere with the acoustics inside the chamber. He was about to repeat the question when Pepper impulsively hugged his bicep close against the firm plumpness of her breasts.

"This is my Secret Place."

Bucher, eyes again wandering over their surroundings, looked back to her quickly, for her tone revealed that this Secret Place was very important to her. Moreover, without being told, he realized her bringing him here made him also something very important, and he cautioned himself to say precisely the right thing in expressing his appreciation.

"How do I like it?" he said slowly, with great deliberation. "Welllll, hmmmmm. It's fantastic, breathtaking, and beautiful, a real good thing to have around, but it's nowhere as lovely and desirable as you are, not even a fraction as delightful as having you around."

She closed her mouth with that peculiar little sound one makes on receiving a light but unexpected blow in the solar plexus, her flawless complexion coloring with pleasure.

"Fibber." She smacked at him playfully in her delight. "Come on. Let's go for a dip."

Though almost desperate to shed the heavy weight of the pack he still carried, Bucher nevertheless stood rooted to the spot, unable to move, scarcely able to breathe as Pepper squirmed free of her sweat-soaked garments in seconds and, with laughter warm and bubbly, flitted past him in a dash through the fissure, disappearing in a long, low dive into the waterfall pouring over the cliff high above. In something less than two minutes later

Bucher, equally *sans tout,* launched himself in a similar dive through the waterfall, plunging into the crystal pool beyond. He surfaced at the lower end of the pool, face to face with Pepper Howard.

"Hi, Badman." Soft arms circled Bucher's neck. "Like my Secret Place?"

"Love it." He slung water from his eyes. "But I expected this pool to be ice cold."

"For several hundred yards before the water pours over the falls it travels over an almost unbroken streambed of limestone that captures heat from the sun. Otherwise it would be much colder."

"But this isn't getting us to the Sinks, is it? Or the Bloody Foreground?"

She studied his hard face quizzically, in silence, head canted to the side like a small bird listening—and inside Bucher became atremble from the impact of her eyes. At last she said: "Well, Badman, I won't blame you for becoming angry, but the only way to reach the Limestone Sinks, or the Bloody Foreground, from my place in one day is by helicopter. If we leave here early in the morning, with luck we should reach the Sinks no later than nine or ten o'clock. And, again with luck, depending on how much time you want to spend at the Sinks, we can stay here again tomorrow night." She pecked the tip of his nose with soft lips. "Are you angry I didn't tell you?"

Beneath the surface, in contrast to the coolness of the water, the fierce body heat of her flesh pressing his sent fumes of mad erotic fancy swirling through Bucher's brain. His throat was brick-dust dry, his tongue clove to the roof of his mouth; he managed to shake his head.

On the verge of speaking further about their plans for tomorrow, Pepper caught herself at the sight of the grinding male agony reflected in the eyes of this hard and bitter man she had loved for years with a pure and secret but despairing and utterly hopeless love, and a tiny spontaneous gasp of joyous surprise escaped her. From the totally feminine charisma inherited abundantly from Mother Eve the patiently smoldering desires of her love instantly were transformed into a seething inferno of ravenous hungers surpassing Bucher's but no longer hopeless and neither to be denied.

"Oh my dearest poor wonderful darling." These whispered words breathed against his lips were husky with wanting. She pointed to the sandy bottom at the shallow edge of the pool, whispering again thickly: "There."

Somewhat adaze from the abrupt and massive onslaught of his emotions, Bucher felt himself drawn gently toward the shallow edge and moved stiffly and woodenly, though motivated by atavistic compulsions older than humanity. He felt himself drawn gently, tenderly, very gently and very tenderly, and gently and tenderly consumed greedily into the seething defile. Behind his clenched eyes inside his head a silent explosion released a dense snowfall of fiery, dizzying sparks that continued to fall relentlessly in seizures of teeth-gnashing, harsh-grunting reality so violent and intense he was but dimly conscious of Pepper's quavering, desperate cries and staccato gaspings.

Time passed. Two hours of it. And two hours and uncounted snowfalls later they made their way back into the huge underground chamber to dress, Bucher in fresh garments from his pack, Pepper in clothing from the enormous plywood box against the chamber's rear wall. The garments they had worn to her Secret Place Pepper tied with a stout cord, then tossed the bundle into the water directly under the falls and tied the free end of the cord to one of the stakes in the wall.

"It'll get the perspiration out of them," she said. "I'll hang them on a line to dry in the morning so we'll have fresh clothes ready when we return tomorrow." With this she began removing from the plywood box canned foods, a self-contained trail cooking kit, blankets and quilts, a huge folded roll of polyurethane, a thick cotton pad, also in a folded roll but smaller, a five-gallon can of gas, another of kerosene, and numerous other items related in some degree to the semi-primitive style of living outdoors. She was handing Bucher a box of matches to start a fire when she dropped the matches and flung herself bodily into his arms, clinging desperately, violent sobs wracking her small frame.

Though taken somewhat by surprise at her unexpected move, Bucher's only response was to hold her close, stroking her glossy black hair. When she at last grew calm after some minutes he continued to hold her until she raised her head, released him, and withdrew a step. Since all tears, per se, are identical, with tears of happiness and tears of sadness having nothing inherent to distinguish them, Bucher, though suspecting the cause behind Pepper's sudden outburst, was not certain of it until he saw the radiant joy wreathing her face, the love for him softly aglow in her eyes.

"Boo, Badman." She wrinkled her nose at him. "But don't expect an apology or an explanation."

Bucher grinned so hard his face hurt. "I don't want an apology and no explanation is necessary." He accepted the matches she had retrieved and again handed him.

"You light both lanterns and get a fire started while I put out some lines. The pool is full of fat trout that're always hungry and we've been out long enough so they'll be biting." She paused, looking at him, head again canted slightly to the side like a listening bird in a manner Bucher was beginning to understand as characteristic of her. "You know something, Badman?"

Bucher lifted the nearest lantern from its hook. "Tell me all about it."

"That book is right."

He struck a match and raised the lantern's chimney. "What book?"

"What book?" She pretended outrage. "That book you saw on my bed while I was showing you Goob's and my birth certificates, sneaky Badman."

From this Bucher knew the book to which she referred, but he didn't know what she meant by saying the book was right. Nor, busy with the lanterns as he was, did he ask. He was soon to learn, however, that her claim the trout were biting was so much the understatement it bordered on the ridiculous, for by the time the fire he built was a bed of glowing coals she had caught and cleaned twenty-one excellent examples to prove it. Cornmeal from a cannister was spread on a length of wide aluminum foil, and as Pepper busied herself with rolling the trout and placing each one in the half-inch of hot fat in the cast-iron skillet on the coals, she tossed Bucher a saucy smile.

"It's right, you know."

"What's right?"

"What that book says you saw on my bed."

Bucher still made no reply. His thoughts were full and powerful of them in the pool and one thought, a conviction really, an irrevocable, immutable conviction, dominated all others: he would never be able to leave these mountains and Pepper Howard behind. Yet, surprisingly, their activity in the pool had little if anything to do with this conviction crystallizing, because it was already crystallized before they had arrived here at her Secret Place. The pool had only served to make his telling her of the conviction more urgent—if it was necessary for him to tell her at all. Less than an hour after their meeting on the trail this morning he felt certain she could read him almost as easily as she could read boldface type.

"Okay," he told her at last. "What is in the book that's right?"

"Later. But it's a promise. It just occurs to me that sex and supper might not be compatible."

"Not compatible with me?" He was hungry enough to eat a wolf.

"Since I've never discussed sex during supper before, it might not be compatible with either of us."

When supper was ready—fried trout, corncakes, and boiled coffee—unquestionably Bucher ate the most delicious meal of his life.

"You like?" Pepper asked after a time, eyeing the heap of fish bones in Bucher's plate with happy approval.

He extended his cup for a third coffee. "I love," he sighed contentedly. "You know something, Pepper? *Every*body ought to have a Secret Place."

"I agree." She nodded, smiling. "I come here when I

can't fight it anymore. Know what I mean? I come here and sometimes stay for a week . . . all by myself. You're the only other person I've ever brought here."

"I know." He followed the thin column of smoke from the coals upward into the darkness with his eyes. According to Pepper it escaped the chamber through a small crack high up in the face of the cliff only a dozen feet directly below the water spilling over into the pool.

"And do you know something, Badman? A moment ago is the first time I ever heard you call me Pepper."

"Really?" Bucher thought for a moment. "You can forget it if you're hoping to ever hear me call you Glycerin Hygroscopic Trihydroxy."

She burst into laughter. "Don't you dare. Never!"

He cast his eyes about the chamber with interest. "Humanity hasn't changed so awful much in the past how-many-millions of years. With few differences you and I might well be caveman and cavewoman squatting in their cave over a pile of bones during the dawn of humanity."

Her throaty laughter tickled his ears delightfully. "The key words are man and woman." She rose and walked to where she had unrolled the polyurethane and covered it with the cotton pad. "And bed."

"Yeah." A warm and wonderful coziness blossomed inside him as he watched her spread quilts and blankets on the cotton pad in finishing their bed. "And sleep."

She smiled engagingly while extinguishing first one then the other of the lanterns, by so doing disclosing that outside darkness had settled over the mountains, then in the dim glow of coals beginning to undress, folding her garments and placing them atop the plywood box. "Phooey on your 'and sleep', Sir Badman. But undress and come on. If you're a good boy I may let you sleep a little."

"There's no need for you to carry everything in that heavy pack tomorrow, only the pack and whatever you think you might need."

Pepper said this up into the heavier darkness after Bucher had banked the fire with ashes, stripped, and was scooting down beside her under the cover. She waited until he was settled, then came to him, resting her head on his shoulder.

"Bucher."

"Yes."

"You fibbed to me about your reason for wanting to find Tony Zubrio, didn't you?"

"Yes." She would learn the truth sooner or later, more than likely, and Bucher figured it might as well be now as some other time. When she did not speak after a reasonable silence, he said: "Aren't you going to ask me the real reason for hunting Zubrio?"

"No. I don't care about the real reason; you'll tell me the real reason if and when it becomes needful for me to know it. I just want you to know you don't have to lie to me. Not ever. Not even if you intend to kill Zubrio because he's the only witness to a crime that could put you in the electric chair."

"I hope Zubrio doesn't force me to kill him, though I will if I must." Then he told her. "Zubrio has on him a notebook containing the addresses of 1168 powerful radio-controlled bombs he and some of his men have planted during the past three years. Each of these bombs is hidden in facilities used by the public and, all other things aside, are a potential threat to thousands of lives all across the country. My job is to get that notebook with the addresses from Zubrio. If it's necessary to kill him to get the notebook, then I kill him."

"Darling. Hush." Pepper shuddered briefly. "You speak of killing a man as I'd speak of going to the mailbox. Besides . . ." she trickled fingertips feather-lightly about his rib cage, ". . . bed is not a place to speak of killing."

With his free arm Bucher flipped aside the top blanket of the two blankets they were under; heat flowed from her body like heat from an oven, and when he did not take her obvious cue she continued, her tone now colored by a puzzling, slightly off-key urgency.

"Bucher?"

"Yes?" The instant he spoke the word it came to him

what the topic of their conversation was about to be, and said: "Oh, yeah."

"Pray tell what you mean by 'Oh yeah'."

He laughed happily, feeling good. "It means we're about to discuss that book that apparently has you fascinated."

"You hit the nail on the head that time, Sir Badman. It has me fascinated. That I won't deny. And also greatly puzzled."

"It's quite a book; lets it all hang out, sort of."

"You've *read* it!?!?" She popped erect as might a jack-in-the-box. Since coming to bed the heat of the banked coals had set fire to a number of twigs and splinters and small pieces of bark mixed with the ashes, and their flickering light did wondrous things to her face. "Why haven't you *told* me?" She goosed him in the ribs and he laughed again, feeling better.

"But I haven't read it."

"Then how do you know it's 'quite a book' that 'lets it all hang out'? In addition to fascinated and puzzled, I'm burning with curiosity and may be also a bit disturbed. Tell me how you know."

"I read a digest of the book, about a hundred and some pages if I remember. I found a magazine in a plane seat on a flight from California to New York last week that included it with digests of three or four other so-called best sellers." This was true. The flight from California had been for the purpose of meeting with White Hat's director concerning Tony Zubrio and his current assignment. "I read it."

"And you weren't fascinated or puzzled or curious or disturbed or . . . anything like that?" She reclined beside him again, head returning to his shoulder. The peculiar urgency was back in her voice. "Not any at all even a little bit?"

"No," he replied honestly, beginning to suspect he knew what she was inching up to. "But the book obviously has great value. In many respects probably. One thing is certain. The prudes, closed-minds, sanctimonious do-gooders, and holier-than-thous, who are always so quick to con-

81

demn as sex perverts any and all who engage in any sex form except the conventional, will be jolted by surprise to learn that the majority of the human race, since there's been a human race, have always practiced those forms they're so quick to condemn. This makes the prudes and their ilk the perverts in a way." A silence slowly crept past. Pepper inhaled a deep, timorous breath, loosing it in a souful sigh that swept across Bucher's chest. When she finally broke the silence her voice was quiet and serious, and about it was that faint fuzziness that precedes sleep.

"Darling, I'm not a prude, nor any of those other types you named, but all my life, since I was old enough to know such sex forms existed, I've wondered about the forms other than the conventional. I want you to explain all about them one of these times. Will you do it? About oral stimulation?"

"Not now?"

"No. Not now. I might go to sleep and I want to hear it all."

A quietness settled over the chamber, the small independent flames from the twigs and pieces of bark at the banked fire were dying out almost as rapidly as they had sprung to life, and before long the gentle rhythm of Pepper's breathing informed Bucher she slept. He cuddled her close, smiling up into the darkness, almost certain she had been on the verge of asking him for a detailed description of cunnilingus and fellatio. He chuckled in spite of himself . . . or maybe it was a demonstration she had her mind set on.

82

CHAPTER SIX

The zesty aroma of boiling coffee drew Bucher from the blissful seclusion of sleep to the realities of the new day. Pepper was already up, hanging on an improvised clothes line their garments kept in the pool all night.

"Up and at 'em, Badman. Time's a-wasting. I found canned bacon and eggs and stuff in your pack. I didn't think you'd want canned corned beef or spiced pork for breakfast and they're the only meats I have left in the plywood box. Come on. Get up. If we scoot fast we can reach Limestone Sinks by nine o'clock."

Bucher dressed hurriedly while Pepper began heaping two metal plates with crisp bacon and scrambled eggs. As he knelt at the pool splashing water on his face he saw through the fissure and to one side of the falls the off-shade darkness of pre-dawn. It was not yet clear enough to distinguish the huge pines surrounding the Secret Place on all sides, but it would be shortly.

"Hungry?" Pepper looked up at him from where she poured two cups of coffee beside the small cookfire.

"Ravenous." Immediately Bucher detected about her a difference this morning; though he was unable to either see it or identify it, it was there, a wonderously delightful difference so real, so present, it was virtually tangible.

She handed him the larger of the laden plates and a cup of coffee, and some minutes later, toward the latter part of the meal, Bucher's eyes found hers over the rim of his cup and the hand holding it commenced a small trembling. Yet again there came to his mind the matter regarding her which he had already settled with himself: either Pepper went with him when he left or he stayed, for he would never leave these mountains without her.

"Badman, why do you look at me so strangely?"

He decided to tell her of his decision at once, then decided against it; there was plenty of time. So he did not answer her question, but sipped his coffee and waited for her to continue. She did.

"Would you like to go by and see our moonshine still on our return here from the Sinks? It's hardly out of the way."

He considered her offer, wondering why she hadn't been more secretive about the illegal moonshine still. When he commented on this she asked:

"Need I have been?"

"No."

"I know that."

"How did you know? I won't buy feminine intuition."

"I know the same way you knew last night at supper that you're the only person I've ever shown my Secret Place." She smiled engagingly. "Must I have a reason for knowing? I just know, that's all." She reached into Bucher's pack behind her and brought forth the battery-powered transistor radio and earplug attachment, the somewhat tenuous means White Hat kept him informed of any recent developments in the Tony Zubrio matter. "Your pack is filled with more unnecessary gear, Badman! Shall we try for some early morning news?"

"Use the standard commercial broadcast frequency," he told her. "We can't get shortwave in here." He watched her fiddle with the radio, fascinated merely by the sight of her and from knowing they were together. He did not have to guess as to the why of this, for he knew already. Knew without guessing. Had known since yesterday—that he was, beyond question, the most incredibly lucky man in the world. It made him feel a bit foolish.

When Pepper found a clear station on the radio Bucher adjusted his hearing to the nasal east Tennessee twang of some rattle-headed morning man extolling the vocal genius of "the late great Hank somebody-or-other," a record he promised to play "right after these hyer friendly words of advice and comfort, neighbors," and plunged headlong into a commercial sympathizing with hemorrhoidal sufferers and suggesting either suppositories or ointment for relief of itching and inflammation; "but if yer bleedin', neighbors, ye ort to see a doctor, naturally, but if—"

Pepper quickly snapped off the set, shuddering delicately with a sound of loathing. Bucher set his plate aside, appetite gone.

"Corporate greed's standard of excellence," she said, shuddering again. "Scrambled eggs and hemorrhoids." She snapped life back into the transistor. "Let's try again, huh?" She began dialing the frequency band control, saying suddenly: "Here's news."

". . . and finally this from Hollywood," the newscaster said in a Standard American accent. "Rock Kordak, another of movieland's greats, star of over fifty hairy-chested, two-fisted roles such as *Hong Kong Hurricane, Killer Kane, Two-Fisted Fury, Badland Territory* and two-time Oscar winner was found in his palatial home in the Hills last evening with a small bullet hole in his right temple and a .22-caliber revolver on the bed beside him. Authorities say Kordak died by his own hand. Kordak's lovely young wife, formerly screenland's sex-symbol Sibyl Silvers, was unavailable for comment, but informed sources told reporters Kordak recently began a series of hormone treatments known to be effective in some instances of chromosomal reversal. According to police, Kordak has no record of homosexuality. Now for the latest weather . . ."

Again Pepper, small jaw clenched, clicked the radio off. In quiet vehemence she said: "Hemorrhoids, homosexuality, and suicide! I think I'd faint and fall back in it if I ever heard one of those dumb-johns report that such and such a number of people attended church last Sunday. Or visited the sick and aged. Or prevented *x*-number of children here in the land of plenty from going to bed hungry at night by buying food with the tax money the government sends overseas in the form of war material. Or—"

"Hey! Hey! Hold on," Bucher laughed, reaching out and tousling her raven locks playfully. "I've already concluded you should've been born a missionary, or a crusader of some sort, or perhaps even a saint, but nobody can remake the world or change humanity. It's all been tried too many times, each ending in failure. The secret is to learn to live with it like it is." He began cleaning up the remains of the meal as Pepper replaced the radio in his pack.

"You're not taking the pack with us to the Sinks, are you, Badman?"

Bucher nodded. "If I don't I'll have to assemble the Super-Hot and carry it openly, which I'd rather not do. But we'll leave the tent, bedroll, cooking gear, and canned foods here. I'll also be taking the radio." He was to listen to White Hat's shortwave frequency for the first time at eight o'clock this morning. Anything broadcast by an announcer named John Franklin was meant for him.

They were ready to leave the chamber, and the Secret Place, when Pepper spoke his name.

"Bucher?"

"Yes."

"I didn't mean to pitch a temper-fit a few minutes ago over that ugliness in the news, but—"

He waited and when she did not continue, asked: "But what?"

"But kiss me, Badman," She smiled happily. "Just once, then we'll go."

CHAPTER SEVEN

An hour later they reached the summit of the ridge above the Secret Place, the ridge opposite the ridge they had descended the day before. Bucher gave her the canteen and drew a forearm across his perspiring brow. On their climb to the summit the sloping forest floor, covered with a thick blanket of pine needles, had created extra work. Each yard advanced was as often as not lost by sliding backward when there was no vegetation within reach to grab and hold on to. A few hundred feet below where they stood, a gigantic natural trough formed by two high ridges angling southeast lay heavily spotted by gradually rising columns of smoke-like blue-gray haze responsible centuries earlier for the name the Cherokees gave to the mountains: Land of the Rising Blue Smoke.

"Look," Pepper pointed to a spot half a dozen yards below them and to the right, and following the direction with his eyes Bucher saw a large clump of the carrot-like Satan's Tea plants, these without white flowers but with an abundance of the small wax-colored berries that reminded him of mistletoe.

"There's a big stand of that horrid stuff near the edge of the clearing down at our Secret Place," Pepper continued, apparently unaware she had changed possessive pronouns. "Did you see it? Well, it's there. And I've promised myself a dozen times I'll destroy it, but I always forget—" She snapped around to face Bucher squarely, large gray eyes troubled. "Bucher?"

"Yes?"

"Bucher?" She gulped involuntarily, a small strangling sound. "Bucher, am I a queer?"

"A what?" He regarded her in surprise.

"A queer? A homosexual?"

"As far as I know you're not? Do you like girls?"

"Ugh! No, not *that* way."

"Forget it then. I take it you don't dig homosexuals."

"I've never knowingly met one. Do you?"

"Depends on what you mean by 'dig'." Bucher studied her expression carefully. She really wanted to know, to understand. "I don't go for sex with men, but I also don't believe in condemning a man or a woman simply because they go for it with members of their own sex. That would be sort of like condemning a person for having cancer or leukemia, or anything else they might have and can't help. Or for being an alcoholic. More often than not there's nothing can be done about that, either, yet society condemns people who drink too much in public. Understand?"

She nodded. "Yes, but last night . . ."

"What about last night?" Bucher did not say so aloud, but he was beginning to wonder at her insatiable interest in a subject, and practice, so common in today's ultra-modern society. But of course Pepper Howard did not live in today's ultramodern society. Hers, with few exceptions, was a society whose morés were largely extinct a hundred years ago.

"I almost asked you to show me something, Sir Bad-man. That's what about last night."

"Why didn't you ask?"

"I was too embarrassed."

"You gotta be kidding. If we were legally married—according to Tennessee law—if I were your husband would you be too embarrassed to ask me then?"

"I—don't know."

"You don't *know?* Goddamnit, that's what's wrong with today's family system! Husband and wife can't communicate! If I were your husband and you couldn't ask me, then who the hell *would* you ask?" His suddenly stern attitude was an attempt to force the matter in the belief that if her curiosity were satiated they could cease talking about it—he had a baddy named Zubrio to locate and neutralize. "Why don't you know?" He studied every feature of her dark-lovely, dear-lovely, sweet-lovely face and silently counted himself the most fortunate of all men. When she made no reply he said: "Come on. Let's get to the Sinks and see if Zubrio is still there."

She made no move, nor even batted a lash for a long, long moment. Holding him with her eyes, their wealth of secret promise created havoc with his emotions.

"Okay, Sir Badman. We'll hurry. But conserve your strength; you'll regret not having eaten all your bacon and eggs at breakfast when we return to our Secret Place. That I vow. Now turn around and let me get that map you showed me yesterday out of your pack. I'll show you where the Sinks and the Bloody Foreground are, just in case."

"I already know where they are—in case of what?"

"In case of anything, silly. Turn around."

The map was a good one. One of the best. It was an aerial-photo map that had been retouched, with contour lines superimposed on it, and all relief features were shown, even the smallest landmarks. The end result was a portion of the earth's surface drawn to scale and portrayed on paper with such meticulous precision and detail that interpretation was little short of instinctive. Pepper's initial response on seeing it the day before had been prompt recognition of numerous places and:

"Boy, I'm glad it doesn't show our still."

Now she spread the map out on the carpet of pine needles, oriented it with the small prismatic compass Bucher handed her, and a second later tapped a spot on it lightly with the tip of a finger. "That right there is Limestone Sinks." A peculiar note of terror, or so it seemed to Bucher, sprang into her voice when she added: "And this here is the Bloody Foreground. We'll have to cross it to reach the sinks."

"Pepper, why are we wasting time here now when——?"

"When we covered all this yesterday? Right, Badman?"

"That's right."

She rose to her feet slowly, carefully, too slowly and too carefully, folded the map and took her own sweet time in replacing it in the pack, then came around in front, regarding him with an enigmatic expression in her eyes. "Okay, Badman?"

"Yeah, sure. I don't know what you're getting at but if you're for it then it suits hell out of me."

"Then perhaps I'm bad for you, Bucher. An article in one of Goob's silly old magazines claims you have the jungle survival instincts of a tiger, but I wonder. Is it I who have somehow unknowingly dulled your survival instincts or have you temporarily dropped your guard for some reason?"

Bucher said nothing. She was about to make a point for his benefit, so he said nothing.

"Look." She extended an arm straight out, pointing down the great natural trough which was still heavily spotted by gradually rising columns of smoky blue haze. "Look carefully now." She moved in close beside him, continuing to point. "See? Near the center of the trough, but just a little bit right of center. You just barely can see it. Can't you? That's Limestone Sinks. Do you see anything unusual?"

"Sure, I see——" Bucher stopped in surprise. "I be damn!"

"Ahhhh. Sir Badman again becomes alert. Now tell me what you see, Sir City-Bred Badman——and please forgive the casual observation that you'd certainly make one very awfully bad moonshine-making partner if you can't even distinguish a column of wood smoke from a column of that blue haze."

By the time she finished speaking Bucher had his pack on the ground and was already assembling the Super-Hot. Pepper hunkered close in beside him and said contritely: "Bucher, please. I didn't mean to sound so superior, or make you feel—however I made you feel."

"Come on," he grinned. "You know darn well I'm furious." He snapped the stock onto the barreled action of the Super-Hot, clicked the two forty-five-round reversible clips in place, tossed the weapon's plastic carrying case back into his pack and stood, slinging the pack over his shoulder and handing the Super-Hot to Pepper.

"Me?"

"You," he told her. "You don't have a weapon, so you get the Super-Hot. The fire down at the Sinks did not create itself. Somebody is down there. Somebody built the fire that makes the smoke and like that. Okay? Is that stone cottage you told me of yesterday the only building there?"

"You think someone is down there?"

"I sure as hell do. And your pigeon message service yesterday said Zubrio was there, though I personally don't believe he came here for nothing except a nature frolic with a couple of broads." Bucher gave Pepper a quick double take. He was mistaken of course, but for one swiftly fleeting instant he thought he saw the ugly mask of raw terror in the depths of her gold-flecked gray eyes. "Come on," he told her. "Let's move, but keep it quiet."

Since their going was all downhill now, they made good time and, all things considered, did so in relative silence. At two minutes before eight o'clock they stopped on the edge of a thicket of pine saplings. As Pepper sat sipping from their canteen, Bucher, transistor radio tuned into White Hat's shortwave frequency and the radio's tiny speaker in his ear, knelt nearby listening closely, listening especially for his code cue, the name John Franklin, which meant that the portion of the broadcast immediately following was intended for Bucher. The name I. M. Kahll, also a code term, was the signal for Bucher to contact White Hat in person with all possible dispatch.

At eight sharp the newscast began, delivered by John Franklin no less and including an account of three powerful nighttime explosions, one each in a leading bank in Atlanta, New Orleans, and Miami. According to authorities each of the bombs had, at some previous time, been placed in a safe-deposit box and apparently had been triggered by remote control. Fortunately no one was injured except one I. M. Kahll, a wino derelict who had been sleeping in an alley behind the bank in Atlanta at the time of the explosion.

All of which, Bucher said to himself as he wound the radio's earpiece cord up and returned the set to his pack, puts an altogether different set of horns on the mule. Yesterday Pepper had told him the only way to reach the Sinks from her house in one day was by helicopter, and since then the idea of renting a helicopter had hovered in the hinterland of his thoughts. There was no question that it would speed things up considerably, though renting a helicopter in this neck of the woods could not be much less of a problem than finding snowballs in hell. Nevertheless, Bucher now told himself silently, somehow he intended to get a helicopter.

Busy as he was with the broadcast, then with returning the radio to his pack, he had not given Pepper any particular notice, naturally assuming she still sat on the pine-needle carpet of the forest floor sipping from the canteen. But she did not, he now noticed. Neither sitting nor sipping but curled on her side in a tight fetal position, Pepper was shaking as though in the grip of a terrible ague, her flawless complexion the ashen pallor of death. Stricken by surprise Bucher lunged toward her, but stumbled over the pack and sprawled to the slippery pine needles underfoot. He recovered instantly, this time reaching her.

"Pepper! For God's sake . . .!" He gathered her tenderly, holding her close with both arms as he knelt there on the ground. "Pepper? What is it? What's wrong?" The sound of his voice seemed to have a restorative effect, for she began to grow quiet at the sound of it, and

92

within a couple of minutes normal color returned to her face and she relaxed, opening her eyes.

"Did I frighten you, Badman?" The question harbored a whimsical lilt, as if attempting to poke fun at herself but failing to pull it off effectively. Bucher released her and reached for the canteen on the ground beside them.

"Yes. Damn right you frightened me. What's this all about?"

She wrinkled her nose at him in a playful grimace. "Don't worry. I'm not subject to fits of any kind. It's . . ." She waved a hand vaguely, then turned a bit, pointing toward a swale behind, and for the first time Bucher noticed the decaying remains of several log structures, most of them appearing to have been dwellings, at some recent time. "That's—Bloody Foreground."

"The place where the people the Rudds killed used to live?"

"Yes. You see, I was the one who found Eagle Tipton and his people the morning after the Rudd raid: that was several years ago. After I returned here from Winston-Salem. Anyway, I got the shakes that day too, just like now. I get them every time I come to Bloody Foreground, though sometimes they aren't as bad as others. This one I think was about the worst since the first one, the morning I found the Tiptons. It's nothing but an attack of nerves. But if you could see what I saw that morning, the way the Tiptons had been slaughtered. And three of the children, not one over five, had been hanged by the neck just so their little toes could barely touch the ground—"

"Easy, easy." Bucher frowned in thought, recalling the Canadian authorities' description of how Tony Zubrio killed the forty-three Eskimos. Apparently sadistic minds ran in the same channels, for Zubrio had killed some of the youngsters in Iglagook the same way the Rudds killed the Tipton infants. The bitter-sour taste of defeat came strong to Bucher's mouth. Any person who mistreated children . . . Bucher cleared his mind, not wanting to think about it further. "I've got some meprobamate in the pack. For the nerves it can't be beat."

Bucher brought her one of the four-hundred-milligram tablets from the pack.

"Will it make me sleepy?"

"No. At least they don't me. You'll never really know you've taken it except that suddenly you won't be uptight anymore. Do you feel like continuing or would you rather rest here awhile?"

"Oh, there's nothing wrong with me, Badman. Let's go on to the Sinks. It's only a little way more."

Bucher gave her a hand up, anxious to get started. Pepper had told him that the Limestone Sinks was nothing more than a lake of several acres in surface area. The only way it differed from any ordinary lake was its location in a vast, deep limestone cavity. During the dry season of the year the surface of the lake sunk as much as twenty-five feet below normal, hence the name. Some years ago a twentieth-century Johnny Appleseed had stopped there long enough to construct a small hut of red clay mud and limestone rock. The hut was seldom used except by mountain folk who came to the Sinks for the plentiful bass and rainbow trout. The area around the hut, and the lake also for that matter, was surrounded by surface limestone and virtually barren of vegetation except for a few scattered pines that had found hungry purchase in places where the stone was thin and broken. The stone hut was built within a dozen yards of the water's edge.

Bucher and Pepper came down through the trees in silence, Bucher leading and keeping to the areas free of underbrush as much as possible, thus reducing chances of anyone at the Sinks detecting their approach by disturbed bushes and the like. And there was somebody at the Sinks. Of this Bucher had no doubt, for already his ears had picked up both male and female voices. Well within the cover of the trees Bucher signaled Pepper and they stopped. He shrugged out of the pack and rummaged through it until he brought forth the compact little 30-power telescope, then maneuvered about back and forth until he found an open place that gave him a clear view of the hut and the immediate area. Carefully, delicately he adjusted the telescope. In actual distance they were three hundred yards from the hut, though when he got a precise adjustment of the 30-power glass it leaped at him, seemingly stopping within arm's reach.

"I be damn!" Bucher muttered in surprise.

"Is something wrong, Badman?" Pepper whispered from beside him.

"Yeah. Bad wrong. It always is when Nino Baragilo and Sergio Toccini are out of the woodwork. They're both down at the hut, along with two blond Amazons who look as if they could hold their own anywhere."

In front of the hut was a large scattering of camping gear, a couple of large packs, a small two-man tent, and a small stack of canned food. Whether the cans were full or empty Bucher could not tell. Nor did he give a hoot. Baraglio and Toccini were the only things at the camp he was interested in. And perhaps the two women as sources of information. And information Bucher was determined to get. Soon. The problem of finding and neutralizing Tony Zubrio, which at first seemed so easy and uncomplicated, was all of a sudden becoming a maze of loose ends. Nino Baraglio and Sergio Toccini were two of the best torpedoes Bucher had ever seen work—he knew them both personally—and neither would be in this neck of the woods, or even this part of the country, if big money was not involved. Of course there was Zubrio's little black notebook listing the locations of the 1168 concealed bombs, which smelled of big money from all angles, but like Q-Boy Kroger, Baraglio and Toccini were west coast hoods. Zubrio operating range, at least in the past, had been confined more or less to the eastern part of the country.

As Bucher watched the four through the glass it came to him that he just might have stumbled onto a Syndicate operation of such magnitude it dwarfed Zubrio's bomb scheme.

"Here." He handed Pepper the glass. "Take a look. Tell me if you recognize either of the two women."

Pepper adjusted the glass to her own sight, made a tiny sound in her throat and lowered it, staring at Bucher in blank dismay. "Why, all four of them are naked as jaybirds."

"Now that you mention it, I do believe you're right," he grinned. "Like to strip and go join them?"

"No!"

"Pssst—take it easy. Don't announce that we're spying on them!"

"But . . . I thought you meant it. About joining them." A certain jealousy edged into her voice. "You might find those two huge women interesting."

"Yeah? Why should I get interested in Model Ts when I've already got a Cadillac in the garage?"

"Hmm, I think I like that."

Bucher shucked his Walther. "Then you stay here on the home front whilst I go hold heated discourse with yon knaves Baraglio and Toccini."

"No."

"Pepper—"

"No!"

"Look—"

"I'll scream."

"Dammit, if you—"

"I'll scream so loud the fish in the lake will turn pale: they won't bite for a month."

"Ahhh, god!" Bucher knew from the stubborn clinch of her small jaw that further argument was hopeless. "Okay, come on. But keep it quiet. And if you trigger that Super-Hot be certain of your aim. I don't want to be stitched up the backbone with 9mm slugs." Bucher started through the timber at an angle that would bring them in behind the stone hut.

The wood smoke that drifted lazily upward looking like the rising blue mountain vapors came from a small but vigorous fire a short distance to the right of the hut, as Bucher viewed it, and it was even closer to the edge of the water than the small stone building. The two hoods and the two blond Amazons were at the fire. Baraglio and one of the women were stretched on a large bedroll far enough away to prevent sparks from reaching them; the other couple were busy preparing a morning meal.

"Bucher." Pepper tugged at his sleeve. "Look."

The hushed fear in her tone caused him to turn quickly, eyes following the direction she pointed in with the muzzle of the Super-Hot. Greasy nausea lurched in Bucher's stomach and a low but blistering oath escaped him. In a small open space some ten yards to the rear of them a man sat straight-backed and rigid against the bole of a tree, his position dictated by the cord that wrapped around about his neck and the tree, and held him erect. Like those at the fire, he too was naked—but he would never enjoy a nude frolic again. Nor anything else for that matter, for he was dead. Bucher reached down and took a part of the flesh of one bicep between thumb and forefinger, pinching it firmly in a rule-of-thumb test to determine the time of death. Rigor mortis was just beginning.

"He got it about the time we were leaving the Secret Place this morning," Bucher whispered.

"D-do—have you ever s-seen it—him before?"

"It's Tony Zubrio."

"Are you sure?" Astonishment colored her words.

"I'm positive: and his death puts a totally different complexion on the entire case. Whoever killed the old goat has the notebook I'm after . . ." He looked toward the four persons at the fire near the edge of the lake. "Guard my back," he told Pepper grimly, "while I go have a talk with Nino Baraglio and Sergio Toccini. And be especially watchful of the two women." He did not add that from his years of experience he knew the female killer to be far more deadly and bloodlustful than the male. "Keep under the cover of these trees—I'd rather they not know of you being with me unless absolutely necessary—and watch my back. Okay?"

"Okay. But you be careful, Badman. You hear?"

Bucher left the trees back of the stone hut, maneuvering to keep the building between him and the foursome to get as near as possible before they spotted him. The fact that Baraglio and Toccini wore nothing did not mean neither had a gun within reach. Bucher would have bet the twenty thousand dollars in the money belt about his waist that both had iron within reach. In the old days, during his years with the Syndicate, he had never known of an instance when they did not. It was an unwritten Syndicate rule of survival.

Nino Baraglio saw Bucher the instant he stepped from behind the hut.

"The Butcher!"

The man froze on the bedroll beside his companion. So did Sergio Toccini. He was in the act of adding wood to the fire when Bucher came into view, and at Baraglio's exclamation he became statue-still, bent toward the fire, a piece of wood extended in his hand. His eyes darted first toward Baraglio, then toward a second double bedroll across the fire opposite the first one, the furtive glances telling Bucher that each man had a weapon in his bedroll.

"You boys take it easy and nobody will get hurt," Bucher told them quietly. "But one false move and you're both dead. Do you read me?"

Toccini straightened slowly from the fire after dropping the wood on it. Baraglio, on the bedroll, lay motionless, nothing moving about the man but his little snake-like eyes.

Both of the women, despite their size, and Bucher estimated both to be at least six feet tall and stacked like Vargas Girls, did not appear to be more than twenty or twenty-one. And they were sisters, to judge by their looks, for the strong resemblance was unmistakable.

"So what are you doing here in the Smokies?" Baraglio growled unpleasantly from the bedroll to Bucher.

"I came to see Tony Zubrio, but it looks as if one of you boys beat me to him," Bucher said.

A wary look appeared around Baraglio's eyes and he and his partner traded quick glances.

"We don't know nothing about Zubrio, Butcher," Toccini snarled, again shooting a sharp look toward his bedroll.

"Then I guess there's nothing left for me to do but to burn you two bastards and be on my way." Bucher looked from one hood to the other, then did the same with the two young women. "And I might as well burn the broads as well. Who do they belong to?"

"I belong to no man," the young woman standing declared in heavily accented English.

"Oh what are we going to do now, Sonja?" cried the girl on the bedroll with Baraglio, and took Bucher so by surprise some seconds passed before he realized she had spoken in Swedish, which Bucher himself spoke with even greater ease and facility than he did Cherokee. "This one who has just arrived and whom they call The Butcher is another of these terrible people."

The one called Sonja stared at Bucher in frigid contempt. "Do not let him see your distress, Olga," she said, also in Swedish. "If he does he may try to use it as a weapon against us in some way. Begin dressing, then we can confront these ogling bumpkins on a more normal footing."

"He is going to kill these two animals who've been holding us captive," Olga wailed tearfully. "And he says he might kill us too."

"Do as I say!" Sonja spat angrily. Both the women had China blue eyes and Sonja's bored into Bucher with a vengeance.

While the two women were dressing Bucher sauntered closer to the fire so he would be out from behind the hut where Pepper could see him. He said nothing, just kept cold eyes on the two Syndicate torpedoes, as the women dressed in hiking trousers and jackets and heavy boots. When they had finished Olga asked timidly:

"W-what do we do now, Sonja?"

"I shall speak to this newcomer in his own language,"

Sonja replied, grimly resolute. "Though how one can define the dialect spoken in these mountains as derived from English I shall never understand."

Bucher said nothing to any of this, nor betrayed that he understood every word. Sonja fixed him with a stern eye, obviously intended to quell and intimidate, and asked in her barbaric English again:

"Sir! If you will be kind enough to let us go, my sister and I will hike out of here." She paused awkwardly a moment. "If you will also give us directions."

Bucher nodded amicably, replying in flawless Swedish: "It will be an honor to be of service to such charming ladies." Whereupon he instantly became an object of boggling from both young women and a throaty snarl from Nino Baraglio. Olga finally sat down on a log near the fire and commenced weeping in relief.

"Oh thank heavens," Sonja gasped in her native tongue, stunned expression fading into a happy smile. "I am Sonja Bjorkvald and this is my sister Olga. Father sent you to find us. Are you with Swedish Secret Service? Your accent is Stockholm." In her relief and excitement she whipped a thick, black cigar from a rucksack near her feet, fired it with a butane lighter, and puffed vigorously.

Bucher did not reply, only stood watching. Once again instinct told him things were not as they seemed: he could expect that as a normal course of circumstances with the two Syndicate hoods, but the girls were a bit more than he had anticipated. His hunch said the two Swedes were the sunbathers who had come into the mountains, ostensibly for a frolic with Tony Zubrio. If he played his cards right he might learn something, providing they knew anything.

"Tell me about your misadventure," he said politely in Swedish to Sonja. "Who killed Tony Zubrio?" She was either too quick for him or else she knew nothing of Zubrio's death for her face revealed nothing but surprise. Neither did Olga's.

"I did not know he was dead," Sonja said quietly, glancing at Baraglio and Toccini in alarm. "Tony was alive the last time Olga and I saw him."

100

"Six or seven days ago," Olga chimed in.

"Who separated you?"

"Two men. One of the Rudd brothers. The other was a gangster. I do not recall his name; if I ever heard it. They took us to some horrid place called Boogerville. We were held there against our will until yesterday, when we convinced these two . . . gentlemen?" . . . She motioned toward Baraglio and Toccini, the gesture accompanied by a sound of thick loathing. ". . . they should help us escape."

"You were kidnapped and taken to Boogerville?" Bucher asked. "And held there until yesterday? What was the ransom?"

Olga's weeping had subsided but it promptly commenced anew in response to this last question. Sonja's reply was more graphic.

"Sex," she told Bucher, puffing vigorously on the black cigar.

"What?" Because of the cigar in her mouth Bucher was not sure he heard right.

"Sex," Sonja repeated. "We were held at Boogerville and used. Rutted on."

"By the two men who kidnapped you?"

"By all the men: eight louts, and almost by one of the women. Eight morons with nothing but sex on their feeble little minds—which we found quite wonderful in a way, except *they never bathe*. One boasted proudly of never having taken a bath in his life."

"Yeah," Bucher commented drily though otherwise not revealing his surprise. "It's hell all right. Where are you girls from?"

"New York . . . Stockholm. Our father is a member of Sweden's delegation to the United Nations. Can you give us directions how to hike out of this horrid place?"

Bucher squatted on his haunches and, keeping the two Syndicate torpedoes well within his range of vision, with his left hand brushed a spot on the ground free of debris and drew a crude map from memory of the aerial-photo map in his pack. "We are right here," he told Sonja. "Now, if you go down this stream leading from the lake to this

101

point, you will come to a main highway. You can hike it until you flag a ride. Do you have money?"

"Travelers' checques, yes." The truth finally dawning on her, Sonja stared. "You are not Swedish?"

Bucher ignored the question as Olga raised her head and viewed him with wet eyes.

"Can you make it to the highway by yourselves?" he asked.

"Certainly. Yes. Of course, easily. You are not coming with us?"

Bucher shook his head. "After a short discussion with Nino Baraglio and Sergio Toccini here, I'm going to Boogerville and take the place apart." He indicated Baraglio and Toccini with a contemptuous gesture, and for whatever effect it might have on the two gunsels he added: "But first I have to bury these creeps."

Sonja and Olga Bjorkvald each snatched a rucksack from the ground and literally raced from the camp. The two Syndicate hoods, Baraglio and Tossini, the former still on the bedroll and the latter still standing near the fire, had that peculiar greenish tint in their coloring related to fear of death. Each knew there was, perhaps, some hope of survival as long as the women were about, but now . . .

"You boys have sixty seconds to either start telling me what I want to know or go for your heaters," Bucher told them. "So make up your minds. If you're not spitting it out by sixty seconds from now I start shooting."

"What the hell you want to know, Butchy?" Toccini whined servily. "You know we'll tell *you*, Butchy, but what is it you're after?"

"Right now I'm after the name of the one who killed Tony Zubrio."

Toccini and Baraglio exchanged brief glances during which Baraglio nodded to the other quickly.

"Sammy Millieto," Toccini said nervously, eyes darting to a spot behind the log on which Sonja Bjorkvald had sat earlier. Already Bucher had seen Toccini shoot fleeting, surreptitious looks at the same spot behind this log, a spot which Bucher was unable to see, and figured Serigo

102

Toccini was about to make the dumb play for a weapon of some sort there.

"Sammy Millieto has been dead for years," Bucher growled, wondering what the hell was going on. "Zubrio killed him over Maria Millieto, Sammy's kid sister."

"Uh-uh," Nino Baraglio shook his head from where he lay on the bedroll. "That was the way it was supposed to look, Tony killing Sammy over Maria, but that was all window dressing. They wanted people to think Sammy was dead so's he could come here to the mountains and work without nobody looking for him for anything."

"What sort of work?" Bucher asked.

"Pot." This from Toccini. "There's a million tons of the stuff here and these dumb hicks don't even know what it looks like, mostly."

"And Q-Boy Kroger is with Sammy?" Bucher asked.

"That's right," Nino Baraglio chortled, in mock camaraderie, the effluvium of his unexplained and abrupt change of attitude a vulgarity in itself.

Bucher did not require a verbal explanation for the change. Sergio Toccini's darting eyes, in flicking half a dozen or so times rapidly toward the stone hut now several yards behind Bucher and to the right, was explanation enough. And if this had not been enough, the danger-warning hackles on the back of Bucher's neck were. Without change of expression, with no warning whatsoever Bucher dropped to the ground, whirling toward the stone hut as he did so, Walther palmed.

Koosh!

The gentle death sigh of the silencered P-38 in Bucher's big mitt was drowned by Nino Baraglio's exultant cry!

"Get him!" As Sergio Toccini dived for his .357 Magnum behind the log Baraglio sprang to his feet clutching a .45 gut-gun taken from under the head of the bedroll. Sammy Millieto, who had emerged from the small stone hut with a .30-caliber carbine could not obey Baraglio's command to "get him" because he had muffed the last chance he would ever have to "get" anybody. The Walther's dum-dum entered his head above the right eye and

exited out the back of his skull with a shower of splintered bone and brains. He was dead before he hit the ground.

Koosh!

Again the Walther's gentle death sigh and Sergio Toccini was also dead before Sammy Millieto hit the ground, upper spine blasted in two with a slug through the throat. Still from the ground, Bucher swung the P-38 toward Nino Baraglio, who was leveling his deadly gut-gun, in time to hear the sounds of dozens of angry bees zip past overhead and see Baraglio's contorted face and head explode into small chunks of flesh and bone and hair. A split-thought later the mindless staccato of the Super-Hot smothered all other sound around the Sinks.

"Thanks." Bucher got to his feet and stood brushing bits of leaves and dirt from his clothes as a white-faced Pepper walked to him gripping the Super-Hot so hard her knuckles were also white.

"I—I k-killed him," she gulped. "I—h-he was about to shoot you and I killed him."

"Easy, easy Ms. Lovely." Bucher took the Super-Hot from her, leaned it against the log near the fire and took her by the shoulders. "Don't let killing Nino Baraglio get to you. His thing was soaking people's clothes in gasoline and setting them afire—while the people were in them— so don't let burning that crud disturb you. You should be given a medal, or canonized, or something similar."

She gulped again, large gray eyes holding his. "You're sure? About the gasoline, I mean. Did he really?"

"He did really. To dozens over the years, so consider yourself as having done a public service. Believe me, you have." He drew her close and kissed her, then said: "Thanks again. It gives a dumb joker like me a good-good feeling to know a girl as lovely as you thinks enough of him to kill a man, even when the man needs killing."

"Liar," Pepper murmured blissfully, no longer evincing any trace of emotional backlash for killing Nino Baraglio. "You make it sound almost like an obligation. What I did, I mean."

104

"Look at it this way: would you rather Baraglio or I live?"

"Oh," she said gravely. "I see." Then: "Why did you let the two women leave?"

"To get them out of the way. I have friends who will pick them up later. What told you they were lying?"

"I overheard your conversation with them, with that one, and—well, look at all the food and gear scattered about, and I'll bet there's more in the hut. If they escaped from Boogerville yesterday why would they escape with a truck load of supplies? Then there are the bedrolls . . ." At Bucher's nod she asked: "Did you notice those too? The bedrolls? Both are doubles and they're new. My guess is they've been here at the Sinks all the time."

"Yeah—mine too." Bucher stared about in concentration. "But why? Right now that's the biggest word in the world—why?" He walked to the gross body of Sammy Millieto and began searching the man's garments for Zubrio's little black notebook. He did not expect to find it, nor did he, and his search of all the other gear and clothes and sleeping bags produced identical results—nothing. Bucher spent no time puzzling over the reason Millieto killed Zubrio, he did not give a damn about the reason. Nor did the fact of suddenly discovering that Baraglio, Toccini, and Millieto were, or had been, involved in Zubrio's operation. Yet there was one factor puzzling him, puzzling him more with each passing minute, and that was the question, what was Zubrio's action? What sort of operation had he headed that required Q-Boy Kroger, Sammy Millieto, Nino Baraglio, Sergio Toccini, the Rudd brothers in Boogerville, plus others probably? What sort of racket had Tony Zubrio built here in the mountains that required the presence of some of the Syndicate's best guns? Whatever it was it had to be big and that was for sure. Damn big. And somehow, for some reason as yet undetermined, Bucher did not buy the fiction about the Syndicate being interested in the marijuana growing here in the Smoky Mountains. True, harvesting it would bring a fantastic return, yet the Syndicate would

105

never send Kroger and the others here to simply harvest pot, because there were too many others on the organization's payroll to do that kind of slave work. And why had Millieto been living here in the mountains for several years? After he and Zubrio put out the fiction that Zubrio had killed Millieto over Sammy's sister, Maria.

"What now, Badman?" Pepper asked quietly, retrieving the Super-Hot from against the log.

"I need a helicopter. What's the best way to go about getting one?"

"A helicopter? Are you serious?"

"I'm serious. You gave me the idea yesterday. Remember?"

Pepper frowned in thought, finally saying: "I suppose it's no problem to rent one, the problem is getting out of the mountains. Reaching an airport, one large enough to have a rental service, will—Wait!" Her face lit up. "What are you going to do about all this?" Her gesture included the three dead bodies at the hut and the one of Zubrio down in the timber.

"Leave them for the buzzards. Why?"

"Then let's go. Let's not waste time getting to the still; it's not far from here, and maybe, just maybe, we'll find one of our runners there. He can get you to a large airport faster than any other means of travel except aircraft. Come on." Without another word she turned and began leading the way toward a low gap in the ridge behind the hut. Bucher followed in silence.

"There's no use in trying to be quiet," she explained when they reached the gap and began descending the heavily wooded slope on the other side. "If the lookouts think we're trying to sneak up on the still they'll figure we're from Boogerville and drop a few rounds our way." On what appeared to be a long-ago avalanche piled up and seeded over by the surrounding forest she took Bucher by the arm and stopped. "Look, Badman." She pointed far out and down. "See that clay-colored streak running from left to right? The one that stops suddenly? Recognize it?"

Bucher recognized the place at once. "It's that graveled clay spur road where I paid off the taxi yesterday."

"Hey. You're pretty good for a city fellow. Can you tell me in which direction is our Secret Place?"

Bucher glanced at his watch, then pointed to their right rear. "That way."

Pepper's surprise made her even more attractive. "But what does your watch have to do with it?"

"It serves as a compass." He patted her gently on the rump. "Let's move it. I need that helicopter."

She gripped the fingers of her left hand with those of her right in a way that brought her thumbs side by side, and using her hands thus as a whistle blew a dull, stuttery blast. From far down in the gorge in the direction they were heading came an answering blast half a minute later. "Now they know we're coming," she said.

In spite of the pack and the Super-Hot, both of which Pepper now carried, Bucher was at times pressed in order not to be left behind, and only when they burst into a large flat area devoid of all underbrush did she slow, taking his arm when he came up alongside. Bucher was slightly taken aback with surprise when he noted the fiercely proud, possessive look on her face and realized he was the cause of it. It had not occurred to him that she might be proud of knowing him, or because of him, or the fact that they were together; nor did he know precisely what their being together signified in the unwritten lexicon of the mountains. Nor about this last did he care. She was his, and his alone, now and forever. They were twenty yards in the flat area when Bucher saw the moonshine still and three men around it.

"My god," he said in unfeigned admiration.

"It's a beauty, isn't it?" Pepper asked, swinging on his arm. "It cooks a thousand gallons of mash at one time. Everything about it's automatic, everything but starting the gasoline motor that powers the generators, and everything but the still itself is in a dugout up there on the side of the ridge—we're in luck, Badman.

107

There's Thunderbird Turner, the best runner we've got. He'll take you to an airport."

Bucher sensed something amiss the instant they reached the immediate still area, and so did Pepper. She hurriedly introduced him to Josh Hawkins and Simon Sipes, both of whom were dressed identically in overalls and blue shirt. Sipes, in Bucher's opinion, did not have about him that hopeless, detached air of a man who had undergone a brutal castration, but Pepper did not permit him to dwell on the matter for she was already introducing him to Thunderbird Turner. The man was perhaps forty and he had shrewd blue eyes. He wore moleskin trousers, a Scotch plaid shirt, and on his head a leather hunting cap.

"Proud to make your acquaintance, Mr. Bucher," Turner said as they shook hands. "We heard what happened at Pepper's place yesterday." He looked at Pepper. "Did Goober actually turpentine Clabber Rudd?"

Pepper nodded as Bucher lifted the pack and let her slip out of the straps. "Who told you?"

"Ike. Dolly Fancher's boy. He left just awhile ago. I'd a-give a thousand dollars to seen that. It's what ort to be done to all them Rudds. Turpentine 'em then blow their brains out. They'll get theirs one of these days."

"Something is wrong here," Pepper said with conviction, looking from Turner to the other two men. Hawkins and Sipes shuffled their feet self-consciously and refused to meet her eyes. "What is it?" A prolonged silence followed.

"It's Lukey Lazrus, Miz Pepper," Thunderbird Turner said at last. "Claimed he just couldn't take it no more. He asked us not to say anything about it to nobody, but I reckon it's over with by now. And he asked us to make sure he was dead before we . . ." Turner looked away, embarrassed. ". . . before we buried him." He pointed to one side. "Yonder." Looking in that direction Bucher saw a pile of raw earth beside a recently dug grave. Turner continued. "Josh here fetched his Bible.

108

He aims to say some words over Lukey when we put him in it."

"Where's Lukey now?" There was a horrified quality about Pepper's voice.

"Up at the dugout."

"H-how'd he do it, Thunderbird?" she whispered hoarsely.

"Satan's Tea. Biled hisself a strong pot of it and took it up to the dugout. He asked none of us to come up for an hour at least."

"How long ago was that?"

Turner consulted his watch. "Nigh on to three hours and forty minutes ago, I reckon. Josh and Simon was going up after him when we heard your signal."

Quickly Bucher took the Super-Hot from Pepper, and leaned it on the pack. Turning her toward him he drew her close, holding her thus, she clinging to him desperately as one after the other massive shudders vibrated through her small frame. No tears accompanied the shaking, nothing but dry, terrible sobs. Bucher waited until she began to grow quiet, then asked the three men:

"How's the quickest way I can get out of here to an airport that rents helicopters?"

Silence—until Thunderbird Turner asked: "You serious?"

"I'm serious. Damn serious. It's worth a hundred dollars to me."

"That'll be Magee-Tyson Airport outside Maryville, 'twixt Maryville and Knoxville. And I reckon my Special Lady is about the fastest thing on wheels hereabouts, but riding with me can be a mite risky. There's a federal man out of Atlanta swearing hisself blue in the face that he's going to run me into the ground next time I get out on the highway with a load of moon. Only this time I won't be taking a load of moon, but I was about to start when you and Miz Pepper showed up. We can leave whenever you're ready."

"Where will I find you when I get back?" Bucher asked Pepper, who had control of herself again.

"Our Secret Place." She spoke without sound, her lips forming the words, then continued aloud: "Kiss me before you go. Folks might as well start learning now as later that you're my man, which means I'll scratch the eyes out of any hussy who sets her cap for you." Oddly, her statement dispelled much of the gloom the suicide of Lukey Lazrus had cast over the place.

"Can you make it back with the pack and the Super-Hot?" Bucher asked her. He wanted to also ask her why Lazrus had taken his own life, but decided against it. Turner would know.

"Sure. This still is much nearer than my house is. I'll be waiting. Now kiss me and go."

CHAPTER EIGHT

Thunderbird Turner's vehicle was in the bushes along-side the graveled spur where Bucher had paid off the taxi the day before, and not even in southern California, which was renowned for its freaky cars, had Bucher ever seen such an automobile as the Special Lady. It looked as if the rear quarter-length of one sedan had been cut off, an identical sedan cut in two at the wind-shield, then the rear remains of this second car welded onto the front remains of the first, the result a home-made limousine of original design. Extremely original design. The tires were wide-treads, racing tires; the interior had been taken out except for the two individual front seats and there was no dash panel.

"Made 'er myself," Turner said with obvious pride, as he and Bucher climbed into the vehicle. "We've clocked 'er at two-twenty, but I don't never rev 'er up that fast on a gravel road. Be sure and fasten your safety belt, Mr. Bucher. I got word before daylight this morning Sam Yates, a county deputy sheriff who won't have no job with the county when the high sheriff hears what he's up to, I got word this morning that Yates is planning to help that tax feller from Atlanta catch me if I made a run into Knoxville, which is the reason I ain't got a load of moon aboard. I got some plans for that tax feller." A grimness crept into Turner's voice. "Him and another son of a bitch killed my kid brother Alec. The other I done dealt with. Name o' Cobbs he was. This one I'll deal with today, the good Lord willing. His name is Parsons, I think. Roy or Ray or something like that,

111

but his last name is Parsons. So that's the reason I say buckle in tight; in case Parsons and that damn Yates gets after us we'll be speeding it up a bit."

Bucher nodded automatically, agreeably, but Turner's words didn't register altogether. Bucher was too anxious to reach Magee-Tyson Airport for a helicopter, and a telephone to contact White Hat, to give much attention to what the other was saying. In truth, since Nino Baraglio, Sergio Toccini, and Sammy Millieto had entered the picture—and wound up dead long with Tony Zubrio—to say nothing of Sonja and Olga Bjorkvald adding a certain amount of confusion, Bucher was honestly concerned about exactly what sort of case he worked on. He'd been in these mountains less than thirty-six hours, yet it seemed as if each successive hour things became more frustrating.

Then there were the three deposit-box explosions in Atlanta, New Orleans, and Miami. If they were the work of Zubrio's men, or someone who knew of Zubrio's scheme to create a Northern Ireland–type of fear and havoc and had already begun operations, then it was patently clear someone in addition to Zubrio had the address list of the 1168 bombs. And why, Bucher demanded futilely of himself, had dumb-john Sammy Millieto bound Zubrio, presumably his boss, to a tree and deepsixed him with a garrote? Why Millieto and why the garrote? True, Millieto was Sicilian-American, and the garrote was a favorite means of execution throughout the Syndicate, but Millieto was third-generation Sicilian-American and during all the years Bucher had known the man before his break with the Syndicate Millieto had never used the garrote in making a hit, always a knife or a gun. The reason for chilling Zubrio Bucher could understand readily enough. Zubrio was getting old, getting along in years, had been on the verge of a rupture with others of the Syndicate hierarchy more than once because of his often high-handed methods and his lust for publicity, and—the most logical reason of all from an underworld point of view—a younger man wanted his position. It was not only entirely possible but quite likely that Zubrio had been ordered hit by the Syndicate. It happened all the time. But why Millieto and why the garrote, when Millieto never used the garrote and when Maria Millieto, his sister, had borne Zubrio two children? Then there was the Lukey Lazrus suicide.

"Why did Lukey Lazrus kill himself?" Bucher asked as Thunderbird Turner switched muted thunder into the Special Lady, almost positive what the man's reply would be. Nor was he mistaken.

"He feared he was turning into a gal-boy, same as Kurt Garfield. Miz Pepper tell you about Kurt Garfield?" He frowned quizzically. "You knowed Miz Pepper long?"

"Years."

"I always knowed that leetle gal had a feller somewheres, on account of every last Tom, Dick, and Harry in these here mountains has tried to cozy hisself up with her and failed. Every dad-blasted one of 'em did, same as if they'd run smack-dab into a brick wall. And I'm here to tell you some of 'em tried hard, too. But she's always sent 'em on their way nice and polite as you please, never hurting a feller's feelings but not having anything like that to do with him, neither. So I figured you must of knowed her a good long while the way she put her mark on you in front of everybody back at the still." Turner's laughter sounded remarkably like the gobble of an asthmatic turkey. "I reckon when word spreads what she did, that now she's got herself a feller, a lot of these hillbilly roosters be coming by to see what you look like."

Turner goosed the accelerator lightly and the deep-throated mechanical thunder of the Special Lady increased.

"We'll stay on the back roads till we get yon side of Sevierville," he said in a loud voice as he steered the Lady on to the gravel road. You see, I done let word out which road I'll be taking the next time I make a run, which Parsons and Yates'll think I'm doing right now,

113

and if they plan to try stopping me—which I'm willing to bet my last dime they do—they'll pick us up on the far side of Sevierville on the way to Townsend. And right before we get to Townsend, while we're dropping down out of these mountains, I'm gonna learn Mr. Atlanta Tax Man Parsons what all Atlanta tax men ort to know but don't hardly ever."

Again Bucher nodded, though understanding little aside from the fact that Turner expected a chase from a federal agent named Parsons and possibly also from a local county deputy sheriff named Yates. When he made no reply Turner again eased his foot down on the gas feed and tinkered with a small plastic knob connected to two wires and taped to the steering post. The Special Lady's mechanical thunder was reduced instantly to no more than a steady metallic purr.

"Built them mufflers myself," Turner said, again proudly. "Built 'em outta stovepipe. Trouble with 'em is, they don't last more'n three or four trips to Knoxville and back."

"How long will it take us to reach the airport?" Bucher asked.

"Thirty minutes. Maybe less. We got a six-lane highway from Townsend on. We'll make good time once we reach it."

They were making good time already, in Bucher's opinion, taking small comfort in recalling Pepper's saying Thunderbird Turner was one of the best drivers anywhere in the mountains. Few drivers managed to maintain a spotless record for all time, and Bucher was beginning to wonder, from the way the landscape was commencing to blur beyond his window, if this might not be an instance when Turner got a blotch on his— and as yet they were still on the gravel road.

"Yonder's the main highway through to Townsend," Turner said, pointing ahead. He braked the Lady down to thirty miles an hour to turn onto the two-lane blacktop highway, and when Bucher noted the way the vehicle acted in making the abrupt, ninety-degree turn

114

he began to understand Turner's pride in it. A couple of minutes later Turner swore explosively in surprise.

"Looky yonder up ahead! That's Dawson's Cut. That yeller coupe and that black seedan are blocking the road. The black seedan is Yates's and the yeller coupe belongs to Parsons. Souped it up hisownself, they say." Again Turner slowed the Special Lady, this time to a crawl.

Half a mile up ahead, where the road lifted upward to go over a steep rise, the construction engineers had made a cut in the top of the rise twenty-five feet deep, the faces of the cut on each side of the highway at a sharp angle. In the center of the cut the yellow coupe and the black sedan were parked bumper to bumper across the road, blocking it. On the near side of each vehicle stood a man watching the Special Lady creep closer.

"Check your seat belts, Mr. Bucher. We're going to give Parsons and Yates a leetle surprise."

Turner used the accelerando technique, the Special Lady gaining speed with each yard advanced, and 150 yards from the roadblock things began to happen too fast for Bucher to keep track of. At that time the Lady was doing better than seventy-five miles an hour in his estimation, there being no speedometer, when Thunderbird Turner pushed the gas feed flat against the floorboard. The home-manufactured vehicle lept forward like a bolt from a crossbow.

Bucher started to shout, to demand what in hell the man had in mind, but he forgot to do so, for suddenly it came to him that in watching Turner he was watching a master at work.

"Hang on!" Turner cried exultantly, changing gears five times in five seconds.

The two men standing in the road on the near side of the two road-blocking vehicles were suddenly frantically, desperately clawing through their cars to the other side and comparative safety, and at sight of their fear

115

Thunderbird Turner loosed a panther-like screech of victory.

Bucher held his breath, at a complete loss as to Turner's plan which, actually, was successfully put into operation and behind them before Bucher was fully aware of what was taking place. When it was over he could not refrain from shaking his head in admiration; no wonder Hollywood coined millions from making movies about the illegal moonshine business.

Fifty yards from the roadblock, while streaking straight toward it like a bat out of hell, Turner deftly peeled the Special Lady to the right off the blacktop and shot around the end of the yellow coupe, climbing the right face of the cut at a sharp tilt that placed Bucher almost directly above the driver for the space of a hearbeat. Then the Lady purred back onto the blacktop some forty yards on the opposite side of the roadblock.

"Whooooooo-*eeeeeee!*" Turner cried as he again went through a lightning-fast series of gears changing and the Special Lady slowed to a fast walk. Then his face contorted in wild laughter. "Wait'll I tell the fellers about this'n!" he shouted in glee, pounding the steering wheel with a balled fist. Abruptly he sobered. "But them fellers ort not to a blocked that road on account of that ain't the way the game is played. Sam Yates put Parsons up to it, the fee-grabbing son of a bitch. He's trying to suck his way into a nice fat federal government job, likely. But when I get back from the airport and tell the county sheriff what Yates done he won't even be a deputy. A man can't get to be county sheriff unless he's a good moonshiner and that's a fact." Turner turned his head around for a look to the rear, as did Bucher. The two blockade cars were lined out on the road now and coming fast, Parsons' yellow coupe in the lead.

"Ahhhhh," Thunderbird Turner signed voluptuously. "Now's where I pay that lowlife for shotgunning a rear tire off of my kid brother Alec's car at better'n a hundred miles an hour. That's something Mr. Tax Man sure ortn't to a done. He likes to play rough, so I'm gonna give him his druthers."

Again Turner applied foot to accelerator and concentrated on the task he had set for himself, and during the next few minutes Bucher witnessed a display of skill at cat-and-mouse with automobiles he would long remember. Turner kept the Lady just around each curve and barely ahead of the yellow coupe, and all the while very gradually increased the speed. He was not talking now, nor laughing, nor looking behind except for quick glances into the rearview mirror, nor anything else except applying himself utterly to handling the Lady—and all the while his accelerando method kept sending the vehicle faster and ever faster.

"Now watch close, Mr. Bucher," he said at last in a loud voice. "Up ahead yonder is what us runners call the drop-off."

Ahead of them stretched a long black ribbon of highway leading upward to a certain point and after that, nothing in sight except the side of a mountain several miles in the distance. By Bucher's guess the Special Lady was doing well over a hundred when it shot past the point where some seconds previously the road had not been visible. He grabbed, for anything, to hold onto, for the blacktop dipped sharply fifty yards beyond the crest going into a tight curve to the right. Had the Lady continued straight ahead they would have wound up in a mangled, lifeless mess at the bottom of a gorge a quarter of a mile deep. Only then, when the Special Lady took the tight curve to the right easily, did Bucher suspect what lay in store for the man in the yellow coupe behind. He also knew why Turner called his misbegotten mechanical Frankenstein the Special Lady, for though lady it would never be, special it certainly was.

Immediately past the right turn, Turner slowed the car to a halt and sat looking back at the crest of the road where the yellow coupe must come. Bucher followed suit, just in time to see the coupe streak across the horizon. Instantly thick black roils of burnt rubber smoke boiled

117

from all four tires, but the brakes did no good. The coupe was coming far too fast. For one tiny pinpoint of time Bucher caught a glimpse of the driver's stricken face, the face of a man who sees his own death in the offing with no hope of escape, as Parsons struggled frantically with the door handle on the driver's side. Like the brakes, his struggles served no useful end, for the vehicle made not even the faintest pretense at turning right as the Lady had done. It streaked off the blacktop without turning a fraction to the right, shot fifty yards out over the gorge, and began to lob end over end, the driver at last opening the door and in his desperation jumping free, falling free, screaming a guttural, mindless scream in salutation to death waiting for him at the bottom of his quarter-mile plunge. Driver and coupe both were dashed to pieces on the boulders in the bottom of the gorge.

Thunderbird Turner's face was sober as the Special Lady drifted down the tortuous road which, at times, was so twisted and crooked Bucher half expected them to meet themselves coming around a curve.

"It ain't a purtty thing I done, Mr. Bucher, but neither Parsons nor the feller with him that day they killed my kid brother Alec had a right to do what they did. Crawled right up behind him in their car and shotgunned his left rear tire with him doing over a hundred. What I did to Parsons, or let him do to hisself, don't help my brother none, but I figure it sorta evens things up a mite." As he talked he kept looking in the rearview mirror. He swore derisively. "There's that ignorant damn Sam Yates behind us. The eejit's so far back he don't know yet what happened to Parsons. Looky behind us now and see what happens." He reached down toward the base of the steering post, grasped the end of a small cable similar to a speedometer cable, and yanked it hard. Behind them Bucher saw inch-long tarpaper nails commence to dribble onto the blacktop; Sam Yates' black sedan would soon be sporting four flat tires. Apparently the man didn't have enough sense to be afraid.

CHAPTER NINE

Less than half an hour after the yellow coupe plunged into the gorge Bucher was dialing his exclusive thirteen-digit White Hat phone number in a booth at Magee-Tyson Airport. He waited impatiently through a series of electronic pops, clicks, and buzzes, after which a quiet voice came over the wire:

"Go ahead."

"This is the Iceman," Bucher said, using his code name. Therefrom he proceeded to relate the situation regarding the case he was on as he saw it, and then he listened. And listened. And listened for the better part of an hour, interrupting on occasion for clarification of some point, but mostly he listened, and when he at last left the phone booth he did so accompanied by a strong yearning to sit and think until he could assimilate the jarring information passed on to him by White Hat. Foremost among his rather confused thoughts, however, was the happy knowledge the dead Tony Zubrio's little black notebook containing the locations of the 1168 bombs was still in the Smokies somewhere. Or at least it had not been used to set off the three deposit-box explosions in the three separate banks in Atlanta, New Orleans, and Miami. These three explosions were the work of a nitwit group of pseudo-revolutionaries calling themselves the Freedom Fighters, who were already in custody. Thus Bucher knew he must return to the mountains, and Pepper—which he had absolutely no intention of not doing, regardless, if only briefly to see Pepper and lay a few very personal plans of his own for the two of them.

According to White Hat, Q-Boy Kroger had been dispatched from the west coast by the Syndicate for the express purpose of hitting Tony Zubrio, bringing with him to lend a hand if necessary Nino Baraglio and Sergio Toccini. Insofar as White Hat had been able to learn, neither this murderous trio nor Sammy Millieto had anything to do with Zubrio's little black notebook and his bombing scheme, which Zubrio had been exceedingly anxious to peddle to some as yet unidentified buyer overseas in order to extricate himself from some unspecified difficulty with the Syndicate hierarchy. Moreover Sammy Millieto's presence in the mountains for the past three or four years had nothing to do with the marijuana growing in abundance there.

Up to this point in White Hat's revelations Bucher had been in familiar waters, more or less, but from thereon he had been completely over his head. What in hell was an itinerant gunslinger supposed to know about haploids, monoploids, gametes, and parthenogenesis? Or how a woman went about getting herself pregnant without ever being exposed?

Tony Zubrio, White Hat claimed, had in some way been responsible for movieland's male sex symbol, Rock Kordak, killing himself, or rather, Zubrio was responsible for Kordak's sex-drive doing a 180-degree turn, because of which Kordak had taken his own life. Moreover, Zubrio had been in some way associated with Teakwood Academy in northern Ohio, which was not an academy in the generally accepted definition of the word, but a private rehabilitation sanitarium for female dope addicts sixteen years old and younger. The girls at Teakwood were under rigid supervision around the clock, there were no males on Teakwood's staff, nor any allowed on the grounds, ever, yet seventeen of the youngsters were pregnant. Parthenogenesis, White Hat ventured, which was known to happen only to certain types of earthworms. Until now.

The fact that Kurt Garfield and Lukey Lazrus committed suicide by drinking Satan's Tea for the same reason Rock Kordak shot himself through the head strengthened White Hat's speculation that Tony Zubrio was behind the entire nefarious plot, and whatever the ultimate goal of the plot was . . .

Bucher massaged his face vigorously with a big mitt, thinking "Jesus Christ!" and in his confusion over all the tangled aspects of this new information he felt somewhat like the marathon runner who broke all records in a grinding twenty-six mile course running in the wrong direction and a day late.

And then there was the agonizing delay because a helicopter had to be flown in from Nashville and serviced before he could rent it. The sun was less than an hour and a half above the western horizon when he at last got free of the airport, lifting gratefully into the late-afternoon light under full power. Twenty minutes later he eased the small craft meticulously down through the lofty pines, bringing it lightly to rest beside the crystal pool of Pepper's Secret Place. During the flight from the airport he had decided it was too late in the day to tackle Boogerville. For that job he wanted several more hours of daylight; stumbling around in a strange place after dark was not his idea of the proper way to approach the Rudd brothers.

In dismounting from the helicopter Bucher's back for a moment was toward the falls and he found himself looking directly at a large clump of the carroty-like Satan's Tea not more than a dozen steps inside the trees; he liked the stuff less each time he saw it. He turned just in time to catch the small, warm, and wriggly body of Pepper as she flung herself at him.

"Shameless hussy," he grinned in delight. "Where are your clothes?"

With her arms about his neck she drew herself up, nuzzling his neck as she spoke. "It's true, Sir Badman. I'm a hopelessly shameless hussy." She shivered and made helpless, mewling sounds as he traced his hands down over her tiny waist. "Careful, Badman. You can't imagine how volatile I am." She nipped his neck playfully. "Darn it, you've been gone *all day long!*"

"Have you heard yet that Thunderbird Turner settled with the other fellow involved in killing his brother?"

"Hush. Hush. Hush." She placed soft fingers over his mouth. "To occupy myself while waiting for you I made a new rule. It's the only rule in effect here at our Secret Place."

"I'll buy it. What is it?"

"You will? Honestly? There's no backing out, now. Once I tell you, you must obey. Do you still buy?"

"I still buy."

"Very well, here it is: We don't talk business here at our Secret Place. Only honeymoon talk. Agreed?"

"Agreed," Bucher replied promptly. "Nothing could be more welcome." It would be easy. Living in the pressure cooker his life had become since quitting the Syndicate, his moments of complete relaxation were indeed rare. So to enjoy these rare moments to the utmost, he had developed the knack of, in effect, temporarily erasing the routine hazards of his life from his mind.

"Now don't forget." She released him and stepped back, and began pulling him after her as she circled the pool to the underwater shelf by which they entered the underground chamber, pointing to a string of trout in the water as they entered. "Which will it be for supper? Trout or canned meat?" She began undoing the buttons of his bush jacket, hands trembling in her desire.

He turned to make the short dash to dive through the falls when he had shed all his clothes, but Pepper caught his wrist and pulled him toward the pallet.

"There's plenty of time," she told him. "Besides, you promised me something this morning."

"Promised you what this morning?" He could not recall having made her a promise.

Her reply to this was simply to look at him in a certain secret way while the pink tip of dainty tongue appeared and toyed suggestively at the center of her upper lip, and though he still did not recall having made her a specific promise he well knew what she was implying he had promised, and also knew she wanted them to pretend as as if they both had made the same promise to each other.

"Right-o." His grain poked fun at her reluctance to express herself in words. "I'll treat."

A settling dusk was visible at an angle between the edge of the fissure that served as a door and the edge of the waterfall when Bucher again stretched full length beside her on the pallet and lay there without speaking, watching her recover. Some minutes passed before she did completely. Again he grinned, though not this time to poke fun but in amazement—Pepper Howard was something different in his experience with women.

"My god." Her voice was hoarse to a whisper. "I died how many times?" But after several slow, deep breaths the glaze began fading from her eyes until at last they focused on him. "You . . . you . . ." She managed to struggle up to a seated position but was unable to maintain it and flopped across him limply. "This is ridiculous." Because of her hoarseness Bucher could barely distinguish the words.

"Come on," he told her, lifting her aside, getting to his feet, helping her to hers. "A few minutes in the pool will do wonders for you. Can you make the dive through the falls?"

She almost did not, yet in the end she did much better than he because in dashing for the falls his foot slipped when he dived and he burst through the falls to hit the pool beyond on all fours, the sight of which served as a tonic on Pepper. She shouted with hoarse laughter. She also lost her footing, making it easier for Bucher, when he reached her, to duck her under.

"Brute!" she cried happily on surfacing, flinging herself at him, clinging tightly, murmuring against his lips. "Badman, you are really something terrific, did you know that?"

"If that co-op moonshine still isn't over five miles from here I bet they heard you screaming," he chuckled, happy over her happiness.

She massaged the base of her throat with one hand. "It hurts."

"Don't use it like a foghorn next time."

"Mmmm, next time." She rolled her eyes as one fainting from ecstasy. "I wonder if I can wait. But I did rave and carry on like all getout, didn't I?"

"Weelllll, you were only expressing your approval."

"Approval. Dear god. There has to be a better word than approval. Isn't there?" She giggled impulsively. "I fear you've made an addict of me. Can one become an addict of that? I almost died each time. Honest. Could it kill a person?"

"It has."

"No!" Her eyes were large, soulful.

"Oh yes. Right in the midst of the goodies the heart gives out. But don't worry. It's always someone with a lot more years than you have and, oddly, it's always men."

In the gathering darkness she looked at him in wonder. "You're telling me the truth, aren't you?"

"Of course. I've never heard of a woman dying of it."

"Well, darn my socks," she said slowly, then quickly: "But men always much older than you too. Isn't it?" She grasped him by the ears and drew his face down to hers. "Darling Sir Badman, if something like that happened to you I'd . . . I'd . . . I don't know what I'd do!" She kissed him lingeringly, tenderly, savoring the titillations their fencing tongues created, at last withdrawing sufficiently to whisper: "You hungry?" then laughed impulsively. "For trout, I mean."

"Not especially. I ate at the airport late this afternoon."

"Oh?" she exclaimed in delight. "Then why don't we forego supper? For a while anyway."

"Good idea," Bucher said blandly. "I'm sure we can think of *some*thing to pass the time."

"Pooh, you better believe it. Do you like the way I kiss?"

"Mmmhmm. You taste delicious."

"W-what?" She seized his ears again, squealing in laughter. "Boy! Don't *you* come up with some ringers, though? Come on, let's go back inside."

"Is one permitted to ask, ma'am, if you have any evil designs in mind for me?"

"Come on. Maybe it's a surprise. But whatever it is, this time I'm treating."

On returning to the chamber from the pool Bucher had lighted one of the gasoline lanterns, turned the flame low, and placed the lantern around the corner of the plywood box from their bed, the result of this a soft light throughout the chamber, with the dimmest over the pallet where they now lay, an hour after their return inside. Pepper, her head on Bucher's shoulder, traced the tip of a finger aimlessly over his bare chest.

"You didn't scream and tear your hair," she pouted, teasing.

"Sheesh! Once more around the block and you'll have to make soup of those trout and feed me with a funnel."

"I hope you're not sleepy."

"Don't you believe it. No man in his right mind wants to go to sleep on a girl like you."

In order to look into his eyes she raised her head off his shoulder and regarded him quizzically, from close range, in the dim light. "You honestly do like me, don't you?"

"I do."

"Because of the way I put out?"

"Because you're who and what you are and because of the way you put out to *me*. There's a difference about you I've never encountered before." This was not exactly what he wanted to say, but he let it pass.

"Careful, Badman. I might get the silly notion you intend to ask me to go with you when you leave here."

"Either you go with me when I leave or I don't leave."

"W-what?"

"Either you go with me when I leave or I don't leave."

"I . . . but . . . we . . ." She paused, inhaling deeply. "You know what you're saying, of course?"

"Of course. I've said it twice and it sounded exactly the same both times. Am I presuming too much?"

"No," she said quietly after a long silence, returning her head to his shoulder once more. "You aren't presuming too much at all." Again silence, then: "Whew! You don't beat about the bush, do you Badman?"

"There's only one problem troubling me." Bucher said this in serious tones.

"Like what?" she asked in quick concern.

"Well, a marriage license isn't as large as a birth certificate, so how the hell will we get Pepper Glycerin Hygroscopic Trihydroxy Howard Bucher on a marriage license? It won't fit."

For the space of a dozen slow heartbeats she continued to think him serious, then felt his laughter coming with her body and sat erect, pummeling him with small fists. "Cur!" she shouted, struggling not to laugh with him. "Lout! Brute! Churl!" but she lost the struggle and collapsed on his chest, squealing with mirth. When they were quiet again, after a time Pepper reclined beside him.

"Come on, Badman. It's a long time before daylight, and I'd like to spend most of the time feeling like a wife by looking at the ceiling over your shoulder. So come on and be about making like a loving husband."

CHAPTER TEN

They were up and dressing at dawn, Bucher readily agreeing with Pepper's suggestion that they fly to the house and have the trout for breakfast there. He would feel much better if she were at home instead of here at the Secret Place while he went to pay a call on Boogerville. For one reason, he wasn't certain how long he would be gone, and for another some half-civilized hillbilly might stumble on the Secret Place while she was here alone. Thoughts of what could happen to her should that occur filled him with a cold dread. So while she returned the bedding, lanterns, and other gear she kept at the Secret Place to the huge plywood box Bucher stowed his pack and 9mm machinegun in the small, four-passenger helicopter, and little more than half an hour after arising he lowered the craft into the back yard at Pepper's home, between the house and barn.

"Pepper." Bucher sat at the kitchen table watching her prepare their breakfast. "Who told you about Goober's tunnel vision?"

"A doctor. Why? Only the real name is lateral blindness instead of tunnel vision. Goob's type of giantism is *acromegalic* giantism. It's caused by tumors on the pituitary gland and as the tumors increase in size they hamper proper function of the inner fibers of the optic nerves, thus interfering with the nerve supply to the retina. This causes—" She stopped, staring at Bucher, puzzlement overshadowing her features. "Darling, why do you look at me so strangely?"

"I didn't know I was. But where'd you learn all this——? You sound like a doctor yourself."

Happy laughter bubbled from her lips, sparkled in her gold-flecked gray eyes. "Thank you, kind sir. I take that as a tribute to the countless hours I've spent studying. I showed you my books. Did you know a medical student must memorize over five thousand names; parts of the human body, diseases, aches, pains, it goes on and on, he must memorize these *and* the definition of each. I have one of the books. I almost memorized them myself thinking I might find a way to help Goob. You think I'm nuts, huh?"

"I think you're wonderful, an angel. What does parthen—partheno—gen—gen—hell, I can't even pronounce it."

"Parthenogenesis?"

"Right! What does it mean? In small words?"

"It means reproduction of kind by the female without being fertilized by the male. It doesn't happen to humans, but a good example would be if I had been pregnant when you arrived yesterday morning. My pregnancy would have been parthenogenetic."

"Yeah? How so?"

Her peculiar expression told Bucher he had committed a no-no of some sort, then she laughed softly in spite of herself.

"I've a good mind not to tell you, lout, if you don't already know . . . Don't you honestly?"

"Go ahead. Tell me for calling me lout."

"I haven't been fertilized until you showed up. Does that make sense?" She permitted a smoldering look to appear in her eyes. Which reminds me, I can turn the trout on real low heat, and my bedroom . . ."

"Hey-hey!" Bucher interrupted, laughing. "Feed me or else I begin coming loose at the seams. I bite when I get that hungry."

"Anyway, now you know what parthenogenesis is."

"And it can't happen to human beings."

"It is impossible to happen to human beings. Only

among lower plants and invertebrate animals. Why are you suddenly interested in parthenogenesis?"

"Pepper, would you believe me if I told you parthenogenesis *does* happen among human beings?"

"I'd believe you if you told me the moon was made of a square block of black mud, but . . ." She paused in stirring spoon-bread batter. "Are you telling me you have proof of a case where parthenogenesis has taken place?" A thoughtful frown creased her flawless brow. "No. There's a mistake somewhere, either intentional or otherwise. Don't misunderstand me, darling. I believe that you believe, but I also believe somebody is hoaxing you. Do you have absolute proof? Positive proof? In the form of physical evidence? Or are you accepting another's word? I'm not arguing. Or trying to be stubborn. Or obdurate. To tell you the truth, I'm fascinated. But let me explain briefly why I think it can't happen to human beings, and if I sould like I'm parroting a medical textbook, well, where else can one find such information?"

"Later, huh?" Bucher showed her both palms. "Feed your starving spouse lest I wither and blow away. We'll get back to the subject another time, I promise, but right now I have a more pressing problem to solve—Zubrio's little black notebook I told you about?—then we'll have the rest of our lives to discuss whatever we like. Okay?"

"Okay, Badman." She placed a large platter of fried trout on the table in front of him, then the spoon bread, the coffee pot and . . ."

"That's enough." Bucher dug in. "Have you got a weapon on the premises?"

"A pump shotgun like Goob's. Why?"

"I'll be gone awhile this morning and I'm taking the Super-Hot. I wanted to know you had some means of protecting yourself."

"Who'd bother me here, for heaven's sake?"

"Q-Boy Kroger and Clabber Rudd might have the other day. They weren't coming for tea."

"Oh. I take it you're going to Boogerville in search of that little black notebook?"

"Where else?"

"And you wouldn't consider taking me along?" She studied him with a mock covert look.

"Don't be ridiculous. I'm not going after tea either." He glanced through a window beyond the stove. The blue mists were lifting, the day coming in full, and before long bright sunlight would eliminate the haze of the mountains completely.

CHAPTER ELEVEN

Half an hour later Bucher lifted the helicopter into the mountain air—unaware that bloodshot male eyes glared at him in nauseous hatred from the ridge above the house until the eyes found Pepper in the yard watching the craft diminish with distance. Then the man began descending the ridge toward the house, eyes frequently darting toward the trim figure of Pepper Howard, who stood watching until the helicopter passed from sight.

On Bucher's aerial-photo map Boogerville was represented by rooftops of nine buildings, which seemed excessive if the Rudd brothers used the place only for making moonshine whiskey. Bucher harbored no illusions about going to Boogerville. Since the appearance of Nino Baraglio, Sergio Toccini, Sammy Millieto, and Q-Boy Kroger, and even with three of these already dead, conceivably there could be three more Syndicate killers, or six, or a dozen, or any number here in the mountains, probably at Boogerville. Though the day before yesterday Q-Boy Kroger, in the company of Clabber Rudd, had informed Bucher he must go to Boogerville sooner or later, his decision had not evolved into an urgency until he and Pepper discovered the corpse of the murdered Tony Zubrio at the Sinks yesterday. A naked corpse, garroted, with no sign of a little black notebook. And because of this, because there had been no little black notebook, a trip to Boogerville became an urgency.

In certain respects the site of Boogerville and the surrounding terrain resembled the topography of the heavi-

131

ly timbered valley wherein lay the Sinks, except in the Boogerville valley there was no lake—nor a limestone expanse to circle it—though the valley was bisected by a tumultuous stream too large to be called a creek and too small to be called a river. Eight of the nine frame buildings of Boogerville sat in two large squares, each forming a corner of a square. The ninth building snugged hard against the base of the wooded ridge five hundred yards on the opposite side of the stream. From his aerialphoto map Bucher knew the place as well as anyone could without having been there, and his plan of procedure was simplicity itself: surreptitiously sneak into the valley, land the hellicopter in tall timber sufficiently far from the hamlet to be secluded, and thence continue on foot, playing it by ear when he arrived at the buildings.

The plan worked so smoothly and perfectly that Bucher was forced to shrug off suspicion, dismounting from the helicopter exactly twenty minutes after leaving Pepper standing in the yard. Methodically he checked his personal weapons: the switchblade, the brass knucks, the ugly, silencered Walther P-38 plus extra, loaded clips, and then checked the Super-Hot, making certain the extra clips for it were also fully loaded. Following the weapons check he walked slowly around the helicopter in continuously expanding circles several times, for he had been fortunate in locating a suitable landing area in a tall, thick stand of pines. Now he sought landmarks by which he could recognize the area from a distance later and, if need be, in a hurry. The landmark he selected was two lofty poplar trees on a rise within fifty yards of the aircraft, the top of one recently singed by lightning, the limbs of the other sporting a tangled curtain of fox-grape vines. Satisfied, Bucher turned toward Boogerville, which lay two miles south.

Due to the absence of a trail, and because he moved through the forest as soundlessly as possible, and therefore of necessity also slowly, he was one and one-half hours reaching his destination. He began approaching the hamlet proper from the north, but when he discerned the buildings ahead through the trees, and saw that he might reach one of the houses from the rear without leaving the cover of the forest, he retreated a quarter of a mile and circled southwest, thus managing to reach unseen the nearest wooden-frame building.

The rear of the house had a door in the center and a foot-long sawn section of tree for an outside doorstep, and equidistant several feet from the door on either side were windows. Neither window wore curtains of any kind. Bucher crept silently up to the window on the right. Previously it had occurred to him Boogerville appeared devoid of all human sound, but on reaching the window he realized this was incorrect for as he hugged the wall beside the window small sounds from inside reached his ears. The sounds were remotely familiar, though due to their originating on the other side of the wall they were too indistinct to recognize—until he peered cautiously through the window. The room was sparsely, crudely furnished with rough, handmade furniture, the walls and floors completely unadorned. Also completely unadorned and locked in frenzied erotic combat were the two sources of the sounds. The man and woman lay on a double bed and within arm's reach had the window been open. And now, of course, it was impossible for Bucher not to recognize the sounds, in *flagrante delicto* as the two were. Yet because they lay from him at an angle, and because he had seen the man but once and then briefly—at the still yesterday—half a minute passed before he recognized Simon Sipes.

Simon Sipes?!?!

Bleak fury flickered across Bucher's hard face, an instant fury over having been deceived, but it departed as quickly as it arrived. He was not the only one deceived into believing Simon Sipes had been brutally castrated by the Rudd brothers. Cautiously Bucher altered his position at the window into one affording a different angle of view, feeling no qualms nor sense of guilt. He only wanted the truth. He got it, *de vistu et tacto; testi-*

culos habet et bene pendentes, and the minute he got it he moved quickly toward the back door of the building. Weasel-faced Simon Sipes had some questions to answer, the double-crossing sonofabitch!

The back door was not locked, which offset the necessity of Bucher kicking it in, and once inside he strode boldly into the bedroom where Sipes & Company were at play. Since there was no garment to grab, he seized Sipes by the neck from behind with one big hand, yanked and half-turned and flung the stunned man against the wall. He slumped to the floor and sat gaping foolishly, too surprised to understand. The suddenly uncovered wench on the bed had presence of mind enough to snatch a corner of a blanket and draw it across her sweaty charms, the while glaring at Bucher severely for the unfulfilled course events had taken.

"What's your name?" Bucher demanded of her harshly.

The timbre of his voice startled her, invoked fear. She swallowed hard. "Bo-Bovina Rudd."

"Bovina, my name is Bucher." He indicated the still dazed Sipes. "Do you love that scrawny, rat-faced runt?"

Her lips moved but produced no sound. Abruptly her eyes switched to Sipes and she stared, her expression gradually reforming into that of one who discovers unexpectedly the person theretofore taken as a friend is a complete stranger.

"No," she at last whispered. Then clearly: "No, I don't love him. Why?"

"I thought you might be able to convince him I'll kill him if he lies to me. Don't you move out of that bed. Understand?"

"If you aim to beat him, Mr. Bucher, he's got a wife and six kids and a bad heart."

"You didn't seem concerned for his wife and kids when I threw him against the wall. Or his heart either." Bucher laced the fingers of his left hand through Sipes's straw-colored hair and hoisted the man bodily to his feet. "Talk, sonofabitch," he snarled into the other's face.

134

"Talk straight and true else I ram a gun barrel down your muzzle and trigger it a few times."

"W-what is it you want to know, Mr. B-Buch—?" Excruciating pain warped the man's pointy features, he gasped in sharp agony, clutching his chest with both hands and sagging against the wall.

"He's got pills!" Ignoring Bucher's warning not to leave the bed, Bovina Rudd flung aside her scant covering and sprang toward the khaki trousers on a chair in the corner across the room. "It's his heart I reckon." Her tone revealed neither sympathy nor condemnation but a certain philosophical understanding and acceptance. After tense moments of plundering the trouser pockets she dropped them and dashed to where Sipes now sat on the floor slumped against the wall, in one hand a small plastic bottle containing tiny pink pills. She held Sipes's jaws pried apart until she dumped several of the pink pills into his mouth. "Now chew, Si," she told the stricken man, who obeyed and at the same time gradually leaned farther and farther to one side until he lay in half-fetal position on the floor.

"Will you help me lift him onto the bed?" the girl asked Bucher. "He'll come out of it after an hour or so; those pills work wonders, seems like."

Effortlessly Bucher lifted the man from the floor to the bed, at once retrieving the Super-Hot from against the wall to stand watching the girl cover Sipes with a blanket, grateful for Pepper and her wifely industry that his masculine proclivities lay subdued, for Bovina Rudd was nothing if not easy on the eyes.

"There now." She retreated a step from the bed. "He'll be all right soon. You were going to kill him for lying to you about what, Mr. Bucher?"

"Who started the fiction your brothers castrated Sipes?"

"Who star—? W-what?" Perplexity wreathed her face. "What brothers? I have no brothers."

"The Rudds aren't your brothers?"

"Oh. I see. Jesus no they're not my brothers. Do I

135

look like a she-gorilla? Big Snort is the local Boogerville god and reigns by brute force, and I fill in as his fourth wife, kind of. On occasion like. Whenever I must or else is the actual truth of the matter."

"And your name isn't even Bovina Rudd," Bucher said testily.

"Why—how'd you know that?" Unabashed delight shimmered in her blue eyes. "I use the Rudd name for convenience when I'm in Boogerville, and for protection from the other throwbacks of humanity here because my so doing inclines Big Snort to consider me another of his private possessions. And nobody in this neck of the woods crosses the local Boogerville god. That simple-minded gorilla himself nicknamed me Bovina in memory of a pet heifer of his that died. How about that? To perpetuate the memory of a cussed cow. No, bless Pete, my name isn't Bovina Rudd. It's Kate Pernod." She glanced toward the man on the bed, voice dropping. "And the brothers Rudd are supposed to have castrated *that* thing?"

"I seem to recall your enjoying the fact that they didn't." Instantly Bucher regretted the oafish, unkind remark.

Without a word Kate Pernod returned to the chair in the corner, from under the khaki trousers took a sleeveless checkered gingham dress and slipped it on over her dry-tobacco-colored hair, motioning for Bucher to follow as she went to the back door. He obliged, also silently, continuing to follow when they cautiously left the building and entered the forest, she leading them into an exceptionally difficult section to travel through afoot: brambles, strewn boulders, poison ivy, sawbriars, and stubborn tangles of underbrush at which Bucher wondered until realizing the rough terrain also made the section the least likely for someone from Boogerville to select for a stroll or to wander into by accident. Only when they were well out of hearing range and from danger of chance discovery did she halt and turn to face him.

136

"You'll have to accept my word for it," she told him quietly, "but I'm undercover for TBI, the Tennessee Bureau of Investigation, Narcotics Division."

Bucher was not as surprised as he might have been, for in light of her secretive conduct he had already begun to suspect her affiliated with some investigative authority. Nevertheless he said: "Why tell me?"

"Because we have quite a file on the dread Butcher at headquarters in Nashville, which includes a goodly amount of solid material garnered from printed media stuff. Your record for putting on ice with a shootout lo these X-many baddies of organized crime is darned impressive, but the reason you give reporters and related vermin for these shootouts—because said X-baddy instigated the shootout when you demanded of him money he owed you—grows a bit thin after several dozen uses. By your own figures the total is almost five hundred million dollars. And nobody lets any number of people owe him *that* much money."

"So?"

"So you do what needs to be done but what no law on the books, nor any authority including the President, can permit being done openly. Who am I to complain if Uncle Sugar finally wised up and acquired for himself a very efficient rat exterminator? It figures. Look at it closely and it figures. In brief, regarding your question 'Why tell me?' I tell you because I'm convinced we're on the same side. If I'm wrong I'm probably dead and don't know it yet, but if I'm right then hooray for me— though I'll wind up dead in the end regardless because nobody gets out of this world alive." She laughed lightly. "Whew! Your turn." When he started to speak she interrupted with: "Oh, about the way you found Simon Sipes and me—"

"Is none of my business," Bucher interrupted in turn.

"Yes, I agree with that. It wouldn't be anyone's business but mine and Sipes's if I'd acted willingly, of my own volition. Oh, I convinced him I was willing, certainly, but . . ." She grimaced in enormous distaste.

137

". . . but that . . . anyway, a woman, almost any woman can lead Sipes over a cliff by shaking her skirts at him, so I finally decided to try. I knew it couldn't be any more revolting than Big Snort, for god's sake. Anyway, what I'm trying to say is that I've been here most of the time for the past twenty-three weeks and I haven't uncovered one tiny shred of hard evidence."

"Of hard narcotics?"

"My superiors think it's here. Somewhere in these mountains and they settled on Boogerville. And I'm convinced they're right but darn me if I can find proof of it. Can a bureaucratic trollop named Pernod ask what the terrible Bucher is doing in the Smokies?"

"Looking for a mobster named Tony Zubrio," Bucher grinned. "He owes me a million, seven hundred thousand."

"Well happy day," she grinned in return. "And welcome, welcome, welcome; boy am I glad to see you. He's been here. Tony Zubrio has. He comes and goes. He'll be back."

"Not this time. He's dead."

"Oh my."

"I found him yesterday morning tied to a tree at Limestone Sinks. He'd been garroted."

"Not you. You always use a g-gun."

"Nino Baraglio claimed Sammy Millieto did it."

"You saw Baraglio also?"

"And Millieto. And Sergio Toccini."

"You did? Honestly? I wonder why they didn't attempt to collect that quarter of a million dead-only reward on your head. Boy, it's a good thing none of *that* trio owes you mon . . ." Her words faded quickly on noting Bucher's expression, her own expression for half a silent minute depicting suspended animation personified. "Th-they *did* owe you money? All th-three of them? And they re-refused to pay?"

"That's right. They refused to pay." Her eyes widened at the brusque edge on his tone.

"Oh no please, *please* don't be offended at me." Con-

138

sciously or otherwise the intake of breath expanded her lungs to the limit, and she released the breath as a sigh of gratitude. "Hooooly Pete—may I call you Bucher? Those three made my flesh creep. When they were around it was like being in close company with spiders. I suppose I should be grateful to Big Snort. They tried to rent me from that gorilla minus-wit Big Snort Rudd, but they tried only once. Boogerville's local reigning god made it unmistakably clear he 'ain't sharin' his heifers with no damn body' unquote."

"What if Big Snort learns of you and Simon Sipes?"

"Then Simon Sipes will, for a fact, get castrated. By Big Snort. With his bare hands. You see, if I'd failed to sweet talk Sipes out of what he knows of narcotics in Boogerville, providing the wormy little runt knows anything, after—how you found us, as a last resort I intended threatening him with telling Big Snort he raped me."

"You're speaking in the past tense."

"I can't very well manipulate Sipes now. Since he knows you're here."

"The dickens you can't. Go back to Sipes now and inform him bluntly that unless he tells you everything he knows about narcotics in Boogerville, or if he mentions me to anyone in Boogerville, you'll swear to Big Snort he raped you. Then if he flatly refuses to cooperate still, tell him I'm waiting outside chomping at the bit to kill him myself."

"Well holy Pete." Kate Pernod looked pained. "Why couldn't I have thought of that? A person can throw herself into a job like mine, with my enthusiasm and dedication, *only* because she dearly *loves* the work—most of it—but sometimes I get slugged by the conviction I'm nothing and will never be anything as an agent except real lousy, honestly. Why couldn't I have thought of that as well as you?"

Bucher admired her sincerity. "Perhaps you haven't had the survival training I have."

"The what?"

"It takes a lot of training to learn instinctively the surest ways of staying alive. Now scoot. Back to Sipes. I'm right behind you until we get close."

He remained in the woods a hundred yards from the house while Kate continued on inside. She reappeared within a minute after entering the house and motioned excitedly for Bucher to join her.

"Will you please just look at what the crumbly little worm has done?" She pointed toward the bed as they entered, a hint of despairing anger tinting the words. "He's gone." With this she looked at Bucher as though she might decide not to believe it. "Now what do we do?"

"How many people are in Boogerville right now?" Bucher asked, welcoming the germ of an idea he felt beginning to form.

"I don't know, but not many. None of the menfolk or you'd never caught me in the bed with Sipes. With the womenfolk it's different. They hang together like grapes when one of them sneaks into another man's bed. But most of the women are gone too, today; out in the mountains gathering berries and other goodies for Big Snort's birthday wing-ding tonight. He's . . ."

"Say that again? About Big Snort?"

"Today is Big Snort's birthday, which one I don't know, and tonight his wives give him a hoedown celebration. I'm supposed to be helping them but—" A combination of terror and revulsion appeared in Kate Pernod's eyes and she tried but failed to prevent Bucher's witnessing the dry, nauseous retch that sprang from her stomach, so she stood there staring openmouthed at him in unpretentious despair until he asked:

"But what, Kate?"

She took a deep and stabilizing breath. "But I'm his current favorite and do as I please—"

"With remuneration exacted later?"

"Yeah." Gagging struck her again by surprise though this time she made no attempt to conceal it. Pity for the girl's plight stirred Bucher's blood, heating it to fighting

140

pitch, yet his voice was controlled when he addressed her.

"Listen carefully. Perhaps I can arrange things so you'll never again be forced into compensating Big Snort Rudd—for anything. Are you game?"

Since Bucher now knew her true feelings regarding the animal who called her his fourth wife, she cared not a whit that he saw tears of blessed relief fill her eyes. "I'm game—for anything that'll help me finish this da-damn j-job and get me out of here."

"Good girl. Now—how many adults are regular residents of Boogerville?"

After a moment's thought she held up one hand, thumb and all fingers spread, saying as she bent down the thumb: "There's Big Snort and his three wives: Sadie, June, and Wanda." Down went the forefinger: "Clabber and his three wives; Ethel, Ruth, and Opal." Down went the next: "El Dude Rudd and his three: Vicky, Alica, and Lotus." Next finger down: "Then there's Jubal Dorn and his four wives, the Rudd sisters; Katherine, Thelma, Abbie, and Betty, and—" Little finger down: "There's Cousin Dan'l Arps and Zelda, Martha, and Nell, his three. And since you encountered those other gangsters at Limestone Sinks there's only one of those left—Q-Boy Kroger. The two women from Sweden left a couple of days ago, Sonja and Olga Bjorkvald."

"Forget those two," Bucher told her. "The sisters Bjorkvald are in jail by now."

Kate nodded but did not question.

"That's twenty-two adults you named who live here. I suppose there're scads of children."

"Oh lord. Around here kids are thick as hair on a dog. They grow on trees in clusters, seems like, under rocks, in the woodwork. Boogerville has kids by the herd. But for the hoedown tonight they'll be confined to one of the houses and kept by some of the pregnant women. Two or three at the time, working in short shifts. As I understand it, the kids are confined to prevent any from getting injured in case fighting and shooting starts. The womenfolk claim it often does."

"It'll start this afternoon, or whenever the men return, if any get in my way. Incidentally, let's get back out in the woods to do our planning. Can you fly a helicopter?"

Kate nodded. "It's part of our training." She turned toward the door. "We'll do just like before. I'll leave the house first to make certain the coast is clear, and you follow."

They spoke little until they were again in the forest, not as deep in as previously but in the same direction and far enough from the hamlet to escape discovery.

"The Boogerville air force is a helicopter," Kate said when they halted. "That's what Q-Boy Kroger calls it. It's his. Did you see that house against the base of the ridge on the side of the stream opposite the other houses? Well, he keeps it in there. He flies in and out of the mountains several times a week, but what he takes out and brings back, or where he goes, no one knows except Big Snort and that beast tells nothing. What was that you said about Sipes's castration?"

"The story is that the three Rudd brothers held Sipes on the ground and castrated him with a pocket knife, and be damned if I can figure why, unless it was told as scare propaganda to keep strangers from venturing into Boogerville."

"No strangers ever come to Boogerville. Never. There isn't one person outside the regular residents that'll be at the hoedown. If I hadn't given Big Snort the eye, as my superiors warned I may be forced to do or ditch the assignment, I wouldn't have been permitted to remain in Boogerville when I first came here weeks ago." A timid smile trembled on her lips. "Bucher, I am literally aching, in physical pain, from curiosity to know how you intend to arrange things so I'll never again be forced into compensating—as you called it in your masculine ignorance though I forgive you—that bestial Big Snort Rudd for anything. Tell me. I hurt to know."

"Whenever the people return, when Big Snort returns, in full view of men, women, and children I'm going to inform Big Snort that I am taking his fourth wife from him and dare him to take her back. Does that ease your aches and pains?"

Kate Pernod simply gaped, dumbfounded, over a minute passing before she remembered to breathe, to recover the wind the plan had knocked from her.

"Oh no-no-no-no-no." The syllables were not spoken, actually, but intoned in a sort of moaning despair. "You can't do that. You don't know that man. He'll kill you! Don't you know that?! He's stronger than an ox, I tell you! An *ox!* He'll rip you apart, to pieces, twist off your limbs, wring your neck, with savor, zestfully——"

"Shhhhh." Bucher placed his open hand near her lips to stem the rise of her voice, for effect saying: "Do you prefer to continue compensating the man?"

"Oh."

"Decide."

"You're insisting I decide?"

"Hell no," Bucher chuckled. "Now here's the way we do it." As before, so was this plan simple enough to appear ridiculous, and when Kate commented on this, marveling, he replied: "The simplicity is insurance against failure." Next he explained in detail how she could find his hidden helicopter if necessary, concluding this with: "Do you have a weapon of any kind?"

"My service pistol; one of the small .38 semiautomatics, also a can of Mace. They're hidden near the house we were in. Uh, Bucher? What then? After you chop off the head of the snake by immobilizing Big Snort, as you call it, then what do we do?"

"Then we disassemble Boogerville, piece by piece if necessary, nail by nail, until we learn what the Syndicate's interest is in the place and until we locate that little black notebook I told you how to recognize by its contents."

"You didn't tell me why locating the notebook is so vital. Is it that top secret?"

143

He told her about the 1168 radio-controlled bombs, virtually all of which were hidden in places frequented by large numbers of the public. "And that's why finding the notebook is so vital. Tony Zubrio carried it on his person at all times, but Tony Zubrio is dead and it wasn't on him when I came across his corpse because he was naked, wearing nothing but his bonds and the garrote that took his life."

"But can you not surmise the garrote sufficient to establish reasonable conjecture and proceed from that to an equally reasonable and valid inference as to who Zubrio's killer might be?"

Bucher attempted to reconcile his back with the rough bark of the tree he sat leaning against as he faced her across a yard or so, and found himself considering Kate Pernod in an entirely new dimension. The girl not only had plenty of everything it took physically, but apparently also plenty of the right stuff between her ears.

"I won't dodge your question or try to lie you an answer," he told her. "But for our kind of work we didn't train in the same school. I simply don't know what the hell you're talking about." The oblique compliment caused her to blush with pleasure.

"Then who among Zubrio's associates would know the value of the notebook and that he carried it on him at all times?"

Bucher shook his head. "But the word is that Zubrio had arrangements to market the notebook to a group of overseas anti-Americans."

"Such as Sonja and Olga Bjorkvald?"

"That's very possible." The same had occurred to him yesterday. "And if they have the notebook we're in luck. Our people were alerted to pick them up yesterday. But the garrote is not a woman's weapon, which means little. Neither are fat black cigars a woman's smoke, but no one had ever explained this to Sonja Bjorkvald. My guess is that Zubrio's killer was a Syndicate executioner. The organization had a hit-contract out on Zubrio and two of the hoods burned yesterday at the Sinks, Baraglio and

144

Toccini, along with Q-Boy Kroger, came here from the west coast for the express purpose of filling it."

"Then there's your answer."

"Huh?"

"Kroger or one of the men killed at the Sinks killed Zubrio, and since Kroger is the only one of the trio remaining alive a reasonable and valid inference indicates Kroger also has the notebook."

"No." Bucher shook his head stubbornly. "I know Q-Boy Kroger. When I rodded the Syndicate's East Coast Division Kroger was one of my personal bodyguards—along with Sammy Millieto who also got burned at the Sinks yesterday—and Kroger is not the garroting kind. I know. And I know Kroger."

"That is immaterial to the case at hand. Anyone could have killed Zubrio; but I say it is valid to assume that Kroger now has the notebook."

"Oh yeah," Bucher said slowly—by god she was right! "I see what you mean. Now I get your point. You say these people, the Rudds and their wives and all go out in the mountains—for what?"

"Hunt ginseng, hunt game, have shooting matches, play mumbly-peg, poker, set-back, make whiskey at the new still location, and do anything else to pass the time. Anything to give them a reason to get away from Boogerville and the kids for a while." She obviously intended to continue the subject further but caught herself. "I've been forgetting something I wanted to tell you. Clabber Rudd won't be at the hoedown, if that's important. He came dashing in from the mountains two days ago and was acting like a man bereft of all human intelligence and looking as though he'd been tilting with thrashing machines. No teeth, one eye, his nose pulverized, his face gashed, his lips shredded to a pulp; Q-Boy Kroger flew him out in his helicopter to a hospital. And even Kroger had a large bandage covering most of his head."

Bucher was about to enlighten her on Clabber Rudd's and Kroger's misadventures of the day before but

145

stopped to listen to a sporadic flurry of distant pistol shots.

"Those shots mean Big Snort and the others are returning to Boogerville," Kate Pernod said hastily, rising to her feet as Bucher did. "Let's hurry to my house."

"You can handle your part of our plan now, can't you?" Bucher asked. "Camouflaging the Super-Hot, the stream, your bath, and all?"

"Don't let it bother you," she smiled with elaborate politeness. "For the vengeance you speak of on Big Snort Rudd I can chew nails with relish."

"Then let's move it."

CHAPTER TWELVE

The house Kate called hers, so designated weeks previously when Big Snort Rudd announced she was remaining in Boogerville as his "feisty l'il heifer number four" was the same house where Bucher had first met the young undercover agent of the Tennessee Bureau of Investigation, and it was in this house where Bucher now stood well back from one of the front windows watching Kate saunter seductively toward the stream bisecting the Boogerville valley. The first phase of Bucher's plan of attack was underway. Kate still wore only the sleeveless gingham dress. Under the towel draped across her arm, along with fresh garments ostensibly for use following a bath in the stream, she carried the fully loaded Super-Hot *sans* shoulder stock, thus converting the murderous weapon into a highly maneuverable twin-grip pistol with an exceptionally long barrel.

Bucher's plan to neutralize Big Snort Rudd, briefly stated, was to attack Rudd's ego through his virility, which properly executed was the one sure way of preventing all-out attack by Big Snort's kinsmen and neighbors and at the same time would open the way for a detailed search of Boogerville to learn what secret operations transpired in the hamlet. Of special interest to Bucher was the low wooden building across the stream at the base of the ridge several hundred yards away, the building Q-Boy Kroger used as a hangar for his helicopter.

Seventy yards directly in front of the houses the lively water of the stream slowed into a pool, and a dozen yards below the pool a single footlog spanned the stream from bank to bank. Watching through the window, Bucher waited until Kate reached this pool and carefully deposited her garments and the machine gun on the bank. An instant later, when she reached for the bottom hem of her gingham dress, he moved quickly to the door and waited. He did not wait long. Kate tossed the gingham dress aside and stood in unclothed feminine splendor erotically disturbing enough to have created havoc among the eunuchs.

"God a'sweet-mighty!" a masculine voice bawled. Looky yonder! Big Snort's newest heifer nakeder'n a jaybird!"

Bucher used this as a cue by stepping out of the house and walking briskly toward Kate, another masculine voice saying as he reached her:

"El Dude ain't lying nuther, Big Snort. Look for yourself. She's nakeder'n ary jaybird—and some feller's feeling and fondling around on her like she's hisn!"

"He is an' I kill the son of a bitch!" a brutal voice rumbled.

At this Kate Pernod, embracing with Bucher as two lovers in a frenzy to further partake of each other, whispered against Bucher's lips: "That's Big Snort."

Bucher released her and they separated, Kate moving toward her garments hiding the Super-Hot as Bucher faced the buildings to see Big Snort Rudd emerge from one of the buildings into the sunlight.

"That's him," Kate said quietly to Bucher, loathing evident in her voice.

Though he was an inch or two taller and several pounds heavier, in appearance Big Snort Rudd was no less Neanderthaloid than his brother Clabber: the same backward-slanting brow, the same small pink eyes constantly ablink and shifting, the same protruding thick lips and forward-thrusting jaw. The man was even dressed similar to the way Clabber had been yesterday when Bucher beat him within an inch of his life.

"Get away from my heifer you son of a bitch!" The

words sluiced from Big Snort's mouth as one as he confidently trotted forward. He was midpoint between the buildings and the stream when Bucher took Kate's .38 semi-automatic from his pocket and squeezed three rapid shots into the air. Echoes of the shots had scarcely faded before Kate straightened from the pile of her garments with the Super-Hot. Big Snort stopped. The people now in front of the buildings, who were beginning to follow Big Snort, also stopped.

"I can hit a fifty-cent piece at a hundred yards eight times out of nine with this pistol," Bucher told the apish Rudd. "One move and I'll drop you, so stand pat till I say move."

"That's my heifer!" Big Snort shouted, disregarding Bucher's words by moving slowly forward, stopping twenty yards away.

"She was yours," Bucher said loud enough for all to hear. "But now she's mine. I'm taking her from you. She claims you're not man enough anymore, that you go to bed only to sleep."

Big Snort's pink little eyes blinked rapidly, his protruding lips snarled in bestial hatred and from behind him came several gloating guffaws, one Bucher recognized as belonging to El Dude; the first to spot the nude Kate—and which informed Bucher his strategy was correct. With Big Snort out of the way the other inhabitants of Boogerville would be no problem.

"You're lying, son of a bitch," Big Snort rumbled threateningly. "That little heifer ain't never been so well stayed with in bed."

"You're the liar yourself!" Kate said angrily, shouting so those at the buildings could hear, her loathing for Big Snort adding conviction to her tone. "You should not be called Big Snort! You should be called Big *Eunuch!*"

"You're *my* heifer!"

Kate indicated Bucher with a nod. "I'm *his* heifer! And he's already proved to *me* that *he's* no *eunuch!*"

"Good girl," Bucher said quietly to the young woman beside him. She was speaking in a language neither Big

149

Snort Rudd nor the people behind him could misunderstand.

"You want her back then you've got to take her," Bucher said. "And if you try I'll give you the same I gave Clabber day before yesterday."

A gasp of glad surprise escaped Kate Pernod, but Big Snort glared harder, more threateningly.

"It was you who turpentined my brother? He claimed it was that eejit Goober Howard."

"I turpentined him," Bucher lied, hoping thereby to remove possible danger to Pepper's young brother when Clabber Rudd returned from the hospital. "I worked him over good with my fists then turpentined him. I haven't decided yet, but I might do you the same after I work you over."

An awed hush had settled over the people at the houses, which now included all adult residents of Boogerville—the children having been herded inside when Bucher fired into the air. But the hush was beginning to be broken with voices of men and women laying bets on the outcome of the confrontation.

"Kate!" a woman in the group called. "Who'll win? Big Snort or the stranger?"

"The stranger, Zelda," Kate called in reply. "His name is Bucher. He's the one who whipped and turpentined Clabber the other day. Bring a bottle of turpentine, Zelda, in case he wants to turpentine Big Eunuch Snort when he whips him."

A screen door banged and again from behind Big Snort came the guffaws, with El Dude Rudd gloating: "The way Big Snort's wives give a feller the eye whenever his back is turned, why, I been figuring for some time something was wrong with Big Snort. But I never figured him to be no out and out eunuch. Dan'l, you been sneaking over in Big Snort's pasture and sporting amongst his heifers? Haw-Haw-Haw!"

"I aim to kill you, stranger," Big Snort told Bucher. "I reckon you know that. Ain't no man laying a hand on that little naked heifer there with you except me."

150

"He already *has* laid a hand on me!" Kate spat, and from the intensity of her loathing for Big Snort Rudd and the ordures he had made her partner to, she continued, holding the Super-Hot chest high so all could witness. "And it was the finest finger you ever saw, Big *Eunuch*. I repaid him with this." For ten or fifteen seconds she gave a realistic enactment of the cooch-dancer's bumps and grinds that brought "Huzzahs!" from several men. "And I intend to keep paying him, Big *Eunuch*! Every time he'll let me! You're no good to a woman, unless to play limp noodles!"

Any time now, Bucher decided, and with silent thanks to the girl beside him. The line Kate was taking had not been included in his plan, but she had speeded things considerably and he was grateful. Bucher was about to speak to Big Snort when a stocky woman with blunt features dashed out from one of the houses and raced across the open space between the buildings and the stream, a quart bottle of colorless liquid clutched to her breast.

"It's Zelda," Kate whispered. "Dan'l Arps's first wife." "She hates Big Snort with a fiendish hate because of the thing he makes her do to him at times in front of the whole community. Her husband is blind and almost deaf, and of course no one here in the community dares tell on Big Snort. They're too afraid. Or were."

Zelda Arps dashed up to Kate, bottle extended. "The turpentine you wanted," she panted. "The bottle ain't hardly full, but they's enough." She shot a glance at Bucher. "You kill that goddamn animal, mister, and I'll do anything in the world for you." With this she turned and raced back toward the group, spitting at Big Snort in passing him.

"Zelda!" Kate called in a loud voice. "Mr. Bucher says if you want he'll make Big *Eunuch* Snort do for you the same Big Eunuch has been making you do for him!"

"Thankee, Mr. Bucher!" Zelda Arps's voice quivered with hate and she brandished both fists toward heaven. "But I wouldn't have that filthy animal's mouth on me!"

Kate swung the muzzle of the Super-Hot toward Big Snort when the man took a step forward. "I'm aching to cut you in two with this machine gun," she gritted. "But I promised Bucher I wouldn't, you slimy creep. He's the only reason you're still alive." In Kate's tone was a lethal quality the man could not understand. In spite of this the man's gigantic ego persuaded him she teased and thereby effected his judgment in that he put pleading into his pink little eyes and held out both hands in supplication, taking another step toward Bucher.

"Aw, sweet l'il heifer—"

Kate tilted the muzzle of the Super-Hot only a fraction and pressed the trigger. Staccato thunder reverberated through the valley, Big Snort Rudd squalled in fright as a dozen or so 9mm slugs zipped past his ear and the roof corner of the house behind him exploded into splinters.

"I'll sweet little heifer you, you depraved son of a—"

"Easy, girl, easy," Bucher said quickly; she had not lied to Big Snort Rudd in telling the man she had promised not to kill him. "Simmer down a little, huh?"

The quivering rage lingered in her reply. "Bucher, I could tell you some of the things he made me do—"

"Good enough, good enough. Talking about it may help. You can tell me later, when this hassle is over."

No I can't tell you later, Kate Pernod gritted to herself. If I did you could never think of me except in disgust, and when this hassle is over I hope in time to create something between us far more acceptable and intimate than disgust.

"And this hassle is about over right now," Bucher told her quietly. Then louder to Big Snort: "Let's have at it, punk. I'm anxious to meet your other women. For damn sure you won't be needing anything but a bed in the hospital when I finish with you."

"And you with that there gun in your hand, feller?" Big Snort displayed both palms. "You're crazy."

Bucher tossed the semi-automatic over his shoulder into the pool behind, saying to Kate: "Kill him in five

152

seconds if he hasn't gotten rid of that .38–.40 you said he wears belted under his overalls."

Rudd snatched out the weapon and flung it with a force that sent it sailing to hundred feet to the right; obviously Kate's burst from the Super-Hot had made a believer out of him where she was concerned. To Bucher, however, whom he presumed to now be without a weapon, he chuckled evilly. "Only one other thing, son of a bitch." His pink little eyes flicked toward Kate. "What about her?"

"She won't gun you down if you best me," Bucher said, knowing he lied, then lied greater to offset the rare possibility Rudd's hatred and bruised ego proved insufficient incentive. "Also if you best me Kate returns to your stables the same sweet and toothsome l'il heifer."

"Awright feller," Rudd chortled fulsomely. "As you said, les' have at it." He began moving forward. Bucher, hands in his coat pockets with fingers laced through the deadly brass knucks, followed suit, saying quickly over his shoulder to Kate: "Warn me when you spot Kroger." After half a dozen medium-length steps Bucher stopped, waiting, for Big Snort Rudd had made the same incredibly stupid mistake his brother Clabber had made two days past: he lowered his head and extended both enormous paws after the fashion of a wrestler seeking to grapple. So Bucher waited.

He had no intention of grappling, or of permitting Big Snort to grapple. Nor did he intend to show Big Snort the mercy he had shown Clabber, which was none. In very truth he would have whipped out the silencered Walther-P-38 under his arm and blasted Rudd's brains out on the spot had he not hoped to cater to the goodwill of the other people in Boogerville—whose goodwill, very obviously, he was obtaining by his present course of action. Therefore Bucher waited until Big Snort Rudd's stupid, lunging tactics brought the man within reach, then Bucher drew from the pockets of his bushcoat both hands armored with the murderous brass knucks and set to work on the other man with all the

153

speed and savagery of the master craftsman of survival he was.

One-*crunch!* Two-*crunch!* Three-*crunch!* Four-*crunch!*

The uncompromising brutality of each sledgehammer blow was vocally punctuated by Kate Pernod's small sounds of delighted approval.

"Kate! We'uns want to come closer so's we can watch better!" It was Zelda Arps. "You all won't get no trouble from us!"

"Don't come any farther than that round-head rock!" Kate pointed to a grapefruit size stone partially buried in the dirt some twenty-five feet away from the two fighting. Bucher was but dimly aware of these goings-on, his attention on Big Snort as he waited for the man to find him again. Big Snort did, and neither his failure to seize Bucher on his initial try, nor one ear torn half off, a four-inch gash along his jaw, and a patch of skin and hair large as a dollar bill missing from his left temple altered his combat tactics one iota. When he got his bearings he waited a moment watching the inhabitants of Boogerville rush forward and stop twenty-some feet away, then again lowered his head bull-fashion, thrust his paws toward Bucher and charged.

Crunch-one! *Crunch*-two! *Crunch*-three! *Crunch*-four!

Bucher retreated a quick step beyond the man's wildly flailing arms.

"OOOOOrrrrGH!" The inarticulate gust of sound from Rudd's throat was primal man's expression of pain and hate, for even if not before, he now had excellent cause for plenty of both. The flesh around his right eye hung by a thin sheet of skin, his right ear was now completely torn off and missing, his nose lay in an odd position favoring his left eye, his upper lip was split through in two places, and there was an ugly gash on the left side of his jaw matching the gash on his right. But he had staying power. Much greater staying power than his brother Clabber had shown.

Exclamations of surprise and wonder and awe, of approval, even a few of rank disbelief came from the rapt spectators, and a quick glance at Kate revealed to Bucher the young woman's fierce joy in Big Snort Rudd's punishment. She also wept openly, unashamed. It was her expression that decided Bucher not to wait for Rudd to find him this time, but move to the attack himself. He did.

Crunch!-Oooff! Big Snort buckled forward from the solar plexis blow, his descending face smashing into the ascending battering-ram that was Bucher's knee. This flung the dazed man erect and Bucher waded in close without mercy, hooking his shots in short, vicious arcs with all his power into Rudd's ribs, each blow accompanied by the whispery crunching of bones. When Rudd began to sag Bucher clubbed his fumbling hands aside and zeroed with devastating accuracy on the man's already battered face, and with each strike there began to flash into Bucher's mind flickers of Pepper Howard shuddering in his arms when she had told him of finding the bodies of the thirteen members of the Tipton family the Rudds had butchered one night. The flickering images of Pepper and recalling the atrocity did nothing in favor of Big Snort's plight.

Bucher deliberately crushed the man's nose, crushed his jawbone after ripping out his teeth, crushed the other bones of his face with the knucks until he was no longer recognizable as the current reigning local god of Boogerville, USA, as Kate had called him several times. Once more Bucher retreated. He had no intention of killing the man. The authorities could kill him if they chose, however. About this Bucher could not have cared less.

"Has he had enough?" Bucher addressed the group in general.

"No he ain't had enough! Kill him! Kill him! Kill him!" This from Zelda Arps, who jiggled in a frenzy of bloodlust in front of the gathering waving a long butcher knife.

Big Snort Rudd simply stood. He could not see, the savagery of the blows received had partially numbed him temporarily, so he simply stood there without moving, too stunned to move, or to know how or why or for what reason to move, victim of his own brute strength and stamina, the stamina all that kept him on his feet. Nor was the stamina of further effect when Bucher placed one foot flat against his paunch and shoved. Rudd toppled over backward to hit the ground and lay spread-eagled, again without moving. Bucher looked to where Kate Pernod stood, still nude, still holding the Super-Hot, still with tear stains on her cheeks but no longer weeping.

"Satisfied?"

She nodded, swallowing hard, then rushed to him, threw one arm around his neck and pulled his head down. Certain of the onlookers were showing signs of applauding before she finally, at long last, released him.

"I'm satisfied." She glanced briefly toward where Big Snort lay. "I no longer want to kill him. I'd rather now he lived."

"Which one is El Dude?"

Kate cased the people a moment, then pointed, calling: "El Dude. Come here. Mr. Bucher wants to talk to you."

"And while I do, you run slip something on, huh? Else I'll be clobbering all the men in Boogerville to protect your honor."

At this Kate Pernod looked at him levelly, recalling the instance of their meeting and him flinging Simon Sipes against the wall—and yet he could still speak of her honor. Of her *honor?* Her honor, dear god?

"Here, I'll take the Super-Hot while you dress."

Kate thrust the gun at him blindly and whirled toward her clothes on the edge of the stream, heart pounding with excitement, eyes stinging from tears of a different cause.

"Y-you want to talk to me, sir?"

Bucher stared at the speaker in surprise. "You're El Dude Rudd?" Nothing Pepper or Goober or anyone else had said to him since arriving in the mountains had indicated El Dude Rudd was an albino, a pure albino, one of the two pure albinos Bucher had ever seen, with every thing about him, skin, hair, nails, gums, everything except his eyes the pure immaculate white of fresh snow. His eyes were bright pink. His facial features otherwise were Neanderthaloid-Rudd, though he was considerably smaller than Clabber, the smaller of his brothers.

"Yessir, I'm El Dude."

Bucher led him aside from the knot of people who had gathered in close around the spread-eagled Big Snort, and they talked. And with one exception, Bucher learned absolutely nothing from the man that Kate Pernod had not already told him. That one exception? Nobody in Boogerville knew anything about what went on between Q-Boy Kroger and Big Snort except Q-Boy Kroger and Big Snort. El Dude swore to it, urged Bucher to ask any or all of the people living in Boogerville. Bucher obliged by asking all at once but they only looked at him blankly and shook their heads and returned their attention to Big Snort.

"I suspected it would be something like this," Kate said to Bucher. "It's hard to imagine a group of people living in such a tiny community as this and not knowing everything that goes on with everybody, but such was the power to inspire fear of their local dethroned ex-god."

"Big Snort ain't human," El Dude said with conviction. "Clabber ain't neither. They're both my brothers but only because I didn't have nothing to do with it. They're warlocks. Both of 'em. Both he-witches. Everybody knows that."

"And you think Q-Boy Kroger is in that building there where he keeps his helicopter?" Bucher asked the albino.

"I know he's there. When he's in Boogerville he don't stay nowhere else but with his helicopter."

"That's right," Kate told Bucher but looking at El Dude. "But I didn't know he was here. When did he come back?"

"About three o'clock this morning. I was out on the

porch when he landed." El Dude tuned an ear toward the subdued buzz of conversation from those around Big Snort, and after listening carefully said to Bucher. "You all better go on away," he whispered to Bucher. "Zelda Arps was eggin' up talk about killing Big Snort on account of what he forced her to do to him in public, so if you stay you're like to see something that ain't pretty."

"You'll have to answer for the Tipton massacre over in the Bloody Foreground," Bucher told him. "You and Clabber and Big Snort if he's alive."

The albino shook his head doggedly. "Mr. Bucher, me and my brothers didn't have nothing to do with that killing of the Tiptons in the Bloody Foreground. Sammy Millieto thought that up. Oh sure, there was a feud between us Rudds and the Tiptons, had been for generations, but it had sort of died down as far as we was concerned. Then Millieto brought in Kroger and three or four other outsiders, fellers with guns, and one night they all snuck up on the Tiptons and next thing we heard here in Boogerville they was all dead. I swear it."

"Don't look at me," Kate told Bucher. "I don't know anything about it. That was way before my time."

"Who can prove what you say?" Bucher asked El Dude.

"Anybody in Boogerville here that was here the night the killing took place, which is all the grown-ups. They know it. They know me and my brothers was here that night, and they'll swear it in court on a stack of bibles high as my head. They will for me. I know that."

Bucher looked at Kate. Her flowered print dress was another simple-cut sleeveless affair, but she now wore a pair of heavy leather moccasins.

She smiled happily. "What's wrong? Am I overdressed?"

"I was about to ask if you wanted to go with me after Kroger." He gave her the Super-Hot. "You seem to handle this pretty well. And if we don't learn what we're after from Q-Boy, we'll think of something else."

They crossed the creek over the footlog and were some yards on the other side when Bucher spoke again. "You've changed, somehow." She had changed since their first meeting, changed enormously and in the manner one who believed in the supernatural could safely assume her to have been gloriously blessed by some miraculous inner transformation.

"Bucher." She stopped and he followed suit, from her tone and expression what she had to say was important to her. "I want you to know something about me," she continued. "I was married at eighteen to a Tennessee Bureau of Investigation undercover narcotics agent who was killed two years later during an investigation. My husband was the only man I'd ever known before coming to Boogerville. But here I suddenly found myself in a position where I must submit to Big Snort Rudd. Then, desperate for information after weeks of zero accomplishment, this morning I seduced Simon Sipes in hopes of grilling, or blackmailing, the wormy runt. I tell you this because it is important to me that you know I'm not a doxy, that I don't go about jumping into bed with men without a reason."

"I haven't given the matter much thought," Bucher told her. "The word 'doxy' doesn't exist in my private vocabulary. Nor prostitute, trull, trollop, whore, wanton, or any of several dozen other synonyms pretending to categorize feminine morality. As for your not 'jumping into bed with men without a reason', which places a person in a worse moral light with himself, coition or killing?

"I—don't understand what you mean."

"I mean which do you consider worse: submitting to a man or killing a man?"

"Oh, heavens. Killing him of course."

"And do you think I go about killing people for no reason, or that my conscience nevers utters a word of protest? I point this out merely to demonstrate that I, of all people, have no right to judge another's morality. As for the way I found you and Sipes—if those fabulous

159

emotions poets define for us as love aren't present, it's really nothing much more than a glandular exercise in friction, is it? The way I see it, with both Sipes and Rudd, you were simply doing your job and nothing more."

"Holy Pete," Kate smiled in admiration. "If you aren't something, though."

"Come on." Bucher indicated the building at the base of the ridge. "There's work to be done."

The end of the huge wooden structure that was their immediate destination faced the stream, the other end blunting against the ridge, and it wasn't until they reached the near end of the building that Bucher saw that the opposite end not only blunted against the ridge, but appeared to have been built into the ridge as if over the mouth of a cave. One of the questions he had neglected to clear up with El Dude was the means whereby Q-Boy Kroger got his helicopter in and out of the building, but when they reached the building and Bucher saw the heavy metal tracks and trolleys barely visible under the inner edges of the eaves, the question was answered. The building, at least this near end of it, had a roll-away roof. The near end of the building also had a small, standard-sized door, which Bucher opened and pushed inward. Nothing but silence greeted the move.

With Walther palmed, and Kate and the Super-Hot bringing up the rear, Bucher silently entered the building. Until then he had not realized how enormous the building really was, for as they stood in the forepart of it, just inside the door, Bucher could see that this first room, or compartment, was easily a hundred feet in length on all four sides. At the far end was a wooden wall reaching from floor to roof and except for being painted red was identical to the door they had just passed through. Between them and this red door stood Q-Boy Kroger's helicopter, a small freighter capable of handling loads of a ton or less, and on each side of the room the walls were stacked high with five-gallon plastic gasoline cans. Above the door behind them Bucher found what he was looking for.

"What is it?" Kate whispered.

"Radio-controlled power unit for opening and shutting the roof from inside the freighter."

"It's so dim in here. So gloomy. I wish we had a flashlight."

"Just take it easy. We'll make it all right."

"I smell something funny. Do you smell it?"

"Funny how?"

"I mean peculiar. An odor that doesn't belong here—but it's very faint. Perhaps it was my imagination. I don't smell it now."

Bucher's eyes were fully adjusted to the lesser light of the building's interior now, and he noticed something oddly out of place on the floor in front of the red door at the far end of the large room. He motioned for Kate to follow and moved silently toward it, realizing before covering half the distance it was the body of a man, of Q-Boy Kroger he discovered a moment later, or more accurately, the shotgunned remains of Q-Boy Kroger, for apparently Kroger had opened the red door to enter the compartment beyond and someone had been waiting on the other side of the door with a shotgun. The full load of double-aught buckshot had caught Kroger on the lower part of the face. Without the bandage covering the wound where Bucher had shot his right ear off, the man would have been difficult to recognize.

"Oh mercy," Kate whispered.

"Know him?"

"Yes. It's Kroger."

"Don't stand in front of that door. I'll shove it open."

Again with the P-38 ready and Kate following hard behind, Bucher moved through the doorway into a much smaller and better-lighted room, the odor attendant to all chemical laboratories everywhere at once filling his nostrils. Yet the room they entered was not a laboratory, but a huge, one-room efficiency living quarters, with bed, table and chairs, a clothes rack in the corner beside the bed, and in the center of the wall facing the door they had entered was a big fireplace in which a log fire danced briskly. Flush against the wall atop a sturdy table on the left of the fireplace, and between the fireplace and a heavy metal door, sat a powerful radio transceiver and above it, extending up to and through the roof overhead, was what appeared to Bucher to be a submarine periscope. In front of the transceiver table was a wheelchair and in the wheelchair sat the hideous caricature of what had once been a large man.

Involuntarily at sight of him Bucher flinched, and Kate Pernod gasped in surprise and compassion. The hands of the man were visible and normal, but the drape and fall of the thick wool blanket covering his legs indicated that the poor devil had very little left to his legs. This applied equally to the man's head from the buttoned collar of his plaid wool shirt upward, for where there once had been a face, that which remained could in no wise be construed to comply with the generally accepted definition of the word. It appeared to have been created of flesh-colored wax by some insane sculptor holding it too close to the fire too long, for all that remained was a single lashless eye, a nasal opening below and to the right of the eye, and a larger, toothless opening that served as a mouth. In short, all that remained of the face of a man was a grisly mass of scar tissue.

The hands on the arms of the wheelchair moved upward and the hideous mass of scar tissue disappeared into a black cloth pullover mask that had one small opening to accommodate the single eye and a slightly larger opening for the mouth.

On a narrow wooden stand beside the wheelchair sat a single-burner hot plate, recently in use to prepare, Bucher assumed, instant coffee or tea or soup or some such, for the kettle on the hotplate still steamed, as did the heavy stone mug on the wooden stand beside the hot plate.

"I have been expecting you with keen anticipation, old friend, and though it humiliates me beyond description for you and the young lady to see me in this tragic

162

state, I nevertheless have been looking forward to seeing you this one last time."

The masculine voice was deep and resonant, each syllable deep, belltoned; each word pronounced with the meticulous accuracy that betrayed the English language to be the speaker's second language, or at least not his native language. Kate made small sounds of sympathy but Bucher's reaction was akin to shock when he realized the speaker and the horror in the wheelchair were one and the same. Gradually, as if drawn by a powerful, unseen magnet, Bucher moved deeper into the room to stop beside the dining table near the center of it.

"But I see now I made a mistake, old friend," the belltone voice continued. "I should never have permitted you to see what remains of my head and face." The honest warmth and friendliness of the voice was unmistakable, and the perplexity of Bucher's expression caused the man to chuckle.

"You call me friend," Bucher said cautiously. "Do we know each other? Have we known each other in the past?"

"You are looking at the living—as yet living—remains of the man who years ago set up a currency pipeline from the US to Europe by which the then crime overlord of the Syndicate's East Coast Division could siphon several hundred thousand dollars each month into his private coffers in Swiss banks overseas."

Already Bucher had lowered the hammer of the Walther and slid the ugly weapon back into its sheath under his arm, and now, as he stood there beside the table in the center of the room, he felt blindly for one of the chairs and dropped into it, stunned by surprise. And now that he knew, he knew also he should have recognized the man by his voice, for nobody in the world had quite the belltone voice of Lars Johannsen, once owner of a drugstore in Winston-Salem, North Carolina, where Pepper Howard had cashiered as Jeanie Brightfeather.

"Lars Johannsen." It was the best Bucher could do right then.

The figure in the wheelchair chuckled again, nodding in understanding. "Yes, Bucher, I'm afraid the creature you see before you is the living remains of Lars Johannsen—and I would invite you to join me in a cup of tea, old friend, except I wouldn't permit you to drink it if you accepted. You see, it's Satan's Tea. *Bucher! Please!*" Johannsen held both palms outward in a gesture of both defense and supplication at Bucher's involuntary start toward his wheelchair, lowering them only when Bucher sank back into his seat.

"Lars, for Christ's sake!" Bucher's voice bore the overtone of one forced to witness a horrifying yet inevitable event, such as the public execution of a friend.

"Bucher, you and I have always subscribed to the belief that a man's life should be his to do with as he will, to enjoy in the manner it pleases him as long as it harms no one, and to dispose of it, to quit living whenever he likes. Well, old friend, for years I've kept this belief shoved in the back of my mind, afraid to act on it because of Pepper. But she's in the clear now—not that she ever wasn't with the authorities—but with you on the scene to protect her she's also safe from the goddamn Syndicate's killers. Though if you hadn't been at her place with her a couple of days ago she, Goober, and Granny all would have been killed by Q-Boy Kroger and Clabber Rudd. Oh yes, I know all about it, and what you did. Nothing happens in these parts that I don't know about—never mind how. I don't have time enough left to tell you and also tell you things you want and need to know . . . such as the whereabouts of Tony Zubrio's little black notebook with the locations of 1168 powerful radio-controlled bombs."

"You know about that?" Bucher was momentarily dumbfounded.

"I know about that, and what you did at the Limestone Sinks the other day. The Bjorkvald sisters came here with Tony Zubrio to pick up the notebook, which

164

Zubrio had given me sometime ago to hold for him—I didn't know what the notebook contained then. Anyway, Kroger and his men learned of the notebook, and that Sonja and Olga Bjorkvald came to buy it for Zubrio's figure, two million in cash. So Kroger wanted the notebook and the two million also. And when Zubrio wouldn't turn it over to him, and the sisters refused to turn over the two million to him—the sisters had hidden the money here in the mountains during a previous sneak visit, Kroger ordered Zubrio and the sisters taken to the Sinks and killed. You and Pepper reached the Sinks not long after Sammy Millieto tied Zubrio to a tree and garroted him; removing his clothes was to help confuse an investigation should his body be discovered before decomposed. Sonja and Olga were next in line for the garrote. The only thing that saved them was that Nino Baraglio and Sergio Toccini wanted to rut on them a while longer."

From Kate Pernod, who now sat at the table with Bucher, came a small sound of loathing.

"I know," Johannsen told her. "Because I also know what you've been going through, Kate Pernod." He gestured toward the periscope above and behind him. "I saw you the day you arrived and I knew it was the beginning of the end of a lot of things around here, because one look at you in comparison to the ignorant cattle in Boogerville would tell you weren't one of them —but you played your part so well it even fooled Kroger and that fiend was hard to fool." He picked up the stone mug of Satan's Tea, swirled the contents about thoughtfully, and set the mug down again.

"Bucher, old friend," he began again, "something tells me I'd better start at the beginning and tell it to you like it was so you won't go charging about wasting time, and then maybe get the wrong answers."

"I'm for it," Bucher replied quickly. "Go right ahead."

"But just this first, then I will. Last night I sent a fee-grabbing deputy sheriff named Sam Yates, who hates you because you were in the car with T-Bird Turner

165

when Turner led Yates's friend Roy Parsons a chase to his death, and who is a scoundrel, a knave, a low-down bastard, and just about everything ugly you want to call him—Sam Yates I'm speaking of—but who is loyal unto crucifixion to me because I've been paying the man a hundred dollars a week for years, with a five-hundred-dollar bonus each Christmas. What I'm trying to tell you is, last night I sent Yates, who took the back trails and on foot, through the mountains with Zubrio's little black notebook and the Bjorkvald sisters' two million dollars, to Pepper Howard. I talked with her via radio not long after you left her place this morning and Yates was there then. She's got the two million and the notebook; my wedding presents to you and Pepper, Bucher."

"My god! Did Yates know he carried two million dollars?" An icy chill trickled up Bucher's spine. A man like Yates would kill a lot of Pepper Howards for two million dollars.

"Of course he knew. I showed him. Except he thinks the two million is counterfeit and the addresses are Syndicate counterfeit drops, so Pepper is safe. As I said, I talked to her after Yates made his delivery." Johannsen swirled the contents of his stone mug again, and again replaced it on the stand. "I've been wanting to do away with myself for years, Bucher," he began slowly. "Ever since I got this way, the night my makeshift lab in the basement of the old Elkhorn Hotel in Winston-Salem, the whole lab mind you, exploded in flame. The fire did this to me, burned the Elkhorn to the ground, killing Pepper's older sister, Mercy Howard, in so doing. Oh yes. Mercy was one of the Syndicate's girls working at the Elkhorn." The belltone voice altered slightly to include a tremor the man could not control. "I'm checking out because of what the fire did to me and because for too many years life has been one unending agony—except for the times I've talked to Pepper on the radio. God bless everything about that girl and all she holds dear, which includes you, old friend, god bless her now and for ever more, and if you so much as let anyone

166

harm a hair of her head I'll come back from hell and you'll never see another minute's peace until you check into hell yourself and I swear it."

"I don't remember a Mercy Howard working at the Elkhorn Hotel in Winston-Salem," Bucher said. He wasn't sure how to do so, but he wanted to speed matters, for he was beginning to suspect that Lars Johannsen's mind was beginning to wander, and he wanted all of Johannsen's information before the Satan's Tea did the poor fellow in.

"Was the Elkhorn Hotel a house?" Kate asked Bucher quietly.

"Yeah. Syndicate bordello."

"Of course you don't remember a Mercy Howard at the Elkhorn," Johannsen said. "Like Pepper's Jeanie Brightfeather, Mercy's alias was Faith Carson. I know. She and Pepper and Goober, all three of them, lived in the spare apartment next to mine up over my drugstore there in Winston-Salem."

It hit Bucher out of the blue, but he gave no sign it had hit him except to say: "And you were Pepper's husband, right?"

"She told you?"

"She told me she was married one morning and her husband died that evening, but she didn't say it was you."

"I wanted to marry her because she was the prettiest thing I'd ever seen. Then I learned that she'd lied about her age to get the cashier's job at the drugstore, said she was eighteen when she was only fifteen. Yes, fifteen. But I wanted to marry her anyway; I was willing to wait because also there was the matter of a goodly sum of money I wanted her to have and could only leave it to her as my wife because otherwise a sister of mine, a real virago, brother, would take the case to the supreme court to prevent Pepper and Goober from getting it. Anyway, we got married that morning and the chemicals in my lab under the Elkhorn exploded that night. No one but Pepper and Mercy knew this, Bucher, for in the United

167

States I was only a pharmacist, but in Sweden I am, or was, a certified chemist and an accredited medical doctor specializing in endocrinology, the study of the function of human glands.

"Anyway, Pepper and Mercy had come to Winston-Salem to find work in hopes of helping their little brother, whom they brought with them and who was already evincing signs of being a bit retarded in certain areas. But there were few jobs available to untrained mountain women, so Mercy, who was nineteen at the time, began at the Elkhorn and later I gave Pepper a job and before long the three of them moved into my spare apartment upstairs above the drugstore and we were living almost as one family. Pepper and her sister were a long time in understanding why I didn't condemn Mercy for working at the Elkhorn. Mercy used the name Faith Carson, by the way. But I've already told you that, haven't I?"

"Sonofabitch," Bucher muttered in surprise. Now he remembered what it was he thought familiar about the girl's photo hanging between the two birth certificates in Pepper's bedroom.

"You remember her?" Johannsen asked.

"I do now."

"Tell me, old friend, Did you by chance know what Pepper thought about you in those days?"

Bucher shook his head.

"She thought you were a god of some sort." There was no rancor or jealously in Johannsen's tone. "I've never known any woman to love any man so utterly, with such absolute devotion, as Pepper loved you. I knew this all the time, I think, but wasn't certain until after the Elkhorn fire. Ah me. Did you know I was manufacturing LSD-25 in my lab in the Elkhorn basement?"

"I didn't even know you had a lab in the basement. Who marketed the stuff for you?"

"The madame at the Elkhorn. Then later Kroger and Millieto. But the fire ended all that. It was Pepper who saved my life that night, who got me into a hospital

168

under the name of John Whitmore, and would have stuck with me, regardless—she's that loyal and she had no hope for herself where you were concerned—but when I learned I was going to live, and learned the sort of nightmare I'd always look like, I had our marriage annulled. Before that though I had made arrangements for her and Goober to be taken care of financially the rest of their lives—a lot of the money from the percentage you paid me for shipping your cash overseas—then I went to a private sanitarium in northern Ohio."

"The Teakwood Academy." Bucher said.

"By god! You manage to keep abreast of things too, don't you? Yes, it was the Teakwood Sanitarium, a retreat for the horribly disfigured such as I was. I later bought the place and, still later, on the face of it, it became a private institution ostinsibly dedicated to the rehabilitation of young female dope addicts. But first, right after I bought it, it was a chronic alcoholics' retreat to come and dry out. After that it became an experimental station for new and far-out drugs the Syndicate made me produce, threatening to harm Pepper if I didn't obey. But by then I was all set up here in the mountains, by Pepper dealing through a third party. She wanted me to work on such things as medicines for preventing birth defects, like Goober's, experiment with plants to produce more and better nutrition, and the like. Her plan was beautiful, and still is beautiful, but it got sidetracked a bit when the Syndicate moved in."

"Does Pepper know this?"

"I don't think she knows the full extent of it. Tell me Bucher, is she pretty?"

"My god man, don't you ever see her?"

"I haven't seen her since we separated and I went to Ohio, and that was almost ten years ago. Tell me, is she pretty?"

"Have you ever seen a young actress named Karen Valentine?"

"Yes; a fine young actress, and so beautiful a man's eyes could ache from simply looking at her."

"Pepper could pass for Karen Valentine's clone, or vice versa."

"*No!*"

"Tell me, Lars, how come the Syndicate located you here and moved in?"

"Well, at Teakwood in Ohio, I was the only monstrocity left when I bought the place, so I took one small wing for myself and converted the remainder of the place, so I took one small wing for myself and converted the remainder of the place into an ultramodern retreat for chronic alcoholics; a place where they could come and dry out in complete secrecy. Secrecy is a number-one prime drawing card for the famous and the infamous alike when it comes to taking the cure. Anyway, one of the first customers was none other than a teenage starlet who later became Hollywood's female sex symbol and also the wife of Hollywood's male sex symbol. I speak of Sibil Silvers, of course, who married Rock Kordak. But when Sibil came to Teakwood at age eighteen she was the tart of an up-and-coming west coast mobster named Q-Boy Kroger, who came to see Sibil while she was at Teakwood, got lost in the corridors, and wandered into my private wing. I had a mask on and he didn't know me but I knew him from Winston-Salem when he worked for you and I was lonesome. We talked. Then, when Pepper set me up down here, one day Q-Boy Kroger and Sammy Millieto show up. Kroger gives the orders and flies out again, but Millieto remains behind to make certain I carry out Kroger's orders. If I refused to carry out Kroger's orders, Pepper paid the price. Kroger let me know that in no uncertain terms.

"Kroger wanted a new kind of LSD. One that could be taken day after day, as alcohol can be drunk. As you may know, LSD-25 can be taken once, or at most twice, a week. Kroger ordered one that could be taken every day, period; the dumb sonofabitch thought you could order a chemical formula like you can a sandwich at a lunch counter. Oh there are a lot of chemicals that one can trip out, or in, or up, or over, or through on, but all, in some form or other, after prolonged usage, por-duce harmful side effects. Whether he knew it or not, Kroger was asking for the same thing mankind has been seeking for thousands of years: a panacea for reality, and by god there is no such panacea! But I've come up with some whoppers in the past three or four years. I had to or they'd harm Pepper."

"How come you to set up shop here in Boogerville?" Bucher asked. "Of all places, why Boogerville?"

"I didn't. There was only this building to begin with. Millieto was here all the time from the beginning, but Kroger also wanted a local, homegrown strong arm, so he had those eight prefab houses brought in by helicop-ter and set up, then found the Rudd clan from around here somewhere close by, I understand, and moved them in here lock, stock and barrel."

"El Dude Rudd claims he and his brothers had noth-ing to do with the Tipton massacre in the Bloody Fore-ground."

"They didn't. They didn't even know about it until it was over and done with. The Tiptons were killed by Nino Baraglio Sergio Toccini, Sammy Millieto, Simon Sipes, and Kroger."

"Simon Sipes?!"

Bucher and Kate Pernod forcefully pronouced the name in unison.

"Surprised, eh?" Johannsen said. "The massacre was Sipes's idea. Rumor would place the blame on the Rudds. Scare propaganda. Kroger wanted it and he got it. Everybody locally knew a feud of sorts had been go-ing on between the Tiptons and the Rudds for genera-tions, and when Q-Boy Kroger began casting about for ways to create scare propaganda in order to keep strangers out of Boogerville and away from what he called his dope factory here, I understand it was Simon Sipes who brought up the plan to wipe the Tiptons out some night and blame it on the Rudds. Sipes also let word get out that the Rudds had castrated him, though Kroger claimed Big Snort was in on this."

"Are you sure Zubrio wasn't in on the Tipton massacre?" Bucher asked, thinking of the forty-three Eskimo men, women, and children massacred in Canada's Northwest Territories in the hamlet of Iglagook. Canadian authorities laid the crime at Zubrio's door, yet there were numerous identical aspects to the separate atrocties, which might well mean the Eskimos had been slaughtered by Kroger.

"Zubrio was at Teakwood at the time of the Tipton massacre," Johannsen said. "I know this for a fact. Once the Syndicate moved into this operaiton here, using Teakwood as an experiment station, Zubrio began also using it as his private harem. As a matter of fact, several other Syndicate wheels do too, and also fly their friends there on weekends for orgies."

"My information claims there are seventeen cases of parthenogenetic impregnation at Teakwood," Bucher said, already suspicious that White Hat's information about Teakwood inmates was in error.

"Uh-uh." Johannsen's black pullover mask gave a negative shake. "Parthenogenesis among humans is not possible. You should have discussed your information with Pepper. That little rascal knows darn near as much about medicine, and especially about endocrinology, as I do. Only one of the accidental formulas I came up with had any drastic effect on anyone other than to trip them out, and this one particular drug, which I call 2-3-4 because it was my 234th complete experiment, has a drastic effect on the male libido in that it reverses the force of a man's sex drive, though I wasn't able to find out how or why. I tried to destroy the formula and almost succeeded, but Millieto, that evil bastard, swiped some of it. How I don't know, but Kroger got the movie star, Rock Kordak, to take some; got it into his system some way, because Kroger's old flame Sibil Silvers was Mrs. Rock Kordak and Kroger wanted her back. He might have got her, too, since 2-3-4 turned Kordak effeminate and he killed himself, except I got Kroger first." He pointed to a single-barrel shotgun on the bed.

"With that. Been planning it for months. Years even. That damn Q-Boy Kroger can't hurt Pepper now because he's roasting in hell!"

"Where is your laboratory, Mr. Johannsen?" Kate asked.

"Behind me. Through that metal door. It's a dandy, too."

"Two men here in the mountains turned effeminate, Lars, Kurt Garfield and Lukey Lazrus. Because of your 2-3-4?"

"That and Simon Sipes. He got some of the stuff from Millieto and gave it to them because he hated them for some reason. A bastard like Sipes is more dangerous than a cocked gun."

"Lars, does the name Bugsy Moline strike a bell with you?"

"He's a west coast *capo;* you know that as well as I do. Did Kroger tell you the day you shot his ear off that he was sent here by Moline to buy marijuana?"

"That's right." Bucher spoke quickly, but without consciously intending to, for a scarcely detectable fuzziness had crept into Johannsen's belltone voice and Bucher had more questions before Johannsen succeeded in killing himself.

"Uh-uh." Again the black pullover mask moved negatively. "Moline is trying to buy a franchise from the Syndicate to harvest all the marijuana here in the Smoky Mountains, but Moline's boys helped Zubrio plant his 1168 bombs, so Moline's days are numbered, just as Zubrio's were."

"I don't understand," Kate said, looking at Bucher.

"Organized crime exists only due to public apathy," Bucher told her, "and if or when Zubrio's scheme was activated this apathy would swiftly metamorphose into fear and outrage which could easily destroy the Syndicate." Bucher returned his attention to the man in the wheelchair. "What about the name 'De Jourist', Lars? A Frenchman. Was he Zubrio's contact man who peddled the scheme in Europe?"

"Peddled it to a Swedish anti-American revolutionary group who call themselves the Liberators; of which Sonja and Olga Bjorkvald were two. These sisters claimed it was the Liberators who scattered a plane load of marijuana seeds through the Smoky Mountains some years ago—to weaken the enemy from within, as it were. That's also the way seeds for this Satan's Tea, this hemlock, got their start in the mountains. Mixed with the marijuana seeds. This particular strain of hemlock is *Conium Maculatum* of the *Umbelliferae* type, and is a native of Asia, not the Western Hemisphere." The man seemed about to continue when a small buzzer sounded and a light came alive on the transceiver directly behind him. He was extending a hand toward the controls when a rash of radio static filled the room and the light went dead, the buzzer silent. Johannsen chuckled. "That was Goober. Pepper lets him tinker with her set at times in order for the boy to learn how it operates. And he's learning."

"How many people in Boogerville know you are here and have been for years, Lars?"

"Big Snort. Kroger told him someone was here, but not who nor why, and gave Big Snort the job of keeping everybody else in the hamlet away. Did you know what went on here, Kate?"

"No. I knew only that the helicopter came and went, but I had no idea it ferried supplies and such for a laboratory. It's . . . this is all so fantastic. It's—unreal. The whole maze—everything." She smiled in gladness. "What a blessed relief *this* case can be marked closed. Your setup here must have cost a fortune, Mr. Johannsen. And the cash outlay to keep it going a staggering sum."

Johannsen did not answer at once and Bucher held his breath, and when the man in the wheelchair did at last reply the fuzziness of his voice was much more pronounced.

"Installation plus first-year's expenses exceeded $1,-300,000." Despite his unique circumstance, there was

174

pride in the words. "And because the Teakwood Academy was in hock to the hilt I couldn't help. But I raised so much hell that the Syndicate picked up the tab for the second year and for each year since. I told Kroger I'd do his filthy goddamn work but gave him to understand that if the Syndicate danced to the music the Syndicate paid the orchestra. Anyway, the wholesale return on the ordinary LSD-25 I had to continue making for the organization averaged ten times the cost of operating this place. And gradually I've been able to pay Pepper back every penny and then some for her outlay that first year. Now you and she also have the Bjorkvald sisters' two million as a wedding present, Bucher." As an afterthought he added. "Though from all the millions I pipelined overseas for you from Winston-Salem, I suspect that in comparison a mere two million dollars is little more than pocket change."

To this Bucher did not reply, but he could feel Kate Pernod's awe like a physical presence. Instead he said: "Lars, why do you suppose Pepper didn't tell me about this lab, about you being here? I didn't know if you were dead or alive, for shortly after the Elkhorn burned I broke with the Syndicate and because of that stayed away from anyone I'd known before the break, for their protection as well as my own. But I can't imagine why Pepper kept all this a secret from me."

"I can imagine why," Johannsen told him, for a third time picking up the stone mug of Satan's Tea. "She told me. She feared for your life if you came to Boogerville and tangled with the Rudds. You see, Pepper thinks it was the Rudds who massacred the thirteen members of the Tipton family, and she does not know the Rudds did not castrate Simon Sipes, that the castration story is nothing but fictitious scare propaganda. And I couldn't tell her it was a hoax, or tell her the Rudds had nothing to do with the Tipton massacre, or tell her a number of other things for fear it might prove dangerous if Kroger and his men discovered she knew of them."

"Is this the reason she does not know the Syndicate has taken over the running of things here?" Kate asked politely. "It somehow seems a bit incredible that she doesn't know."

"I try to keep it from her, or did, but now that Bucher is here it makes no difference. Syndicate goons won't dare touch her when he's around." Johannsen quickly quaffed the Satan's Tea in the stone mug, and both Bucher and Kate averted their eyes when he poured more from the kettle on the hot plate. "I hope I don't embarrass you, Bucher, Kate, but I've hungered for this hour during so many years of anguish and agony. Please try to understand, please try to forgive me if I seem to gloat over having at last succeeded."

"How much of that Satan's Tea does it take to do the job, Lars?" Bucher was pleased that he could talk of the other's death with casual *savoir faire*.

"Normally one swallow of ordinary strength tea, but this cup I just poured myself is my second. Now that the blessed occasion has finally arrived after years of excruciating patience I'm as eager and excited as a kid headed for the circus." Carefully he flourished aloft the stone mug. "This Satan's Tea is so gentle. It does the job with no pain or nausea or bloodletting. It's a real gentle killer, Bucher." Belltone laughter boomed from behind the black pullover mask. "Y'know something, old friend? I feel good all over, like a miracle about to happen." He brought the stone mug to the larger hole in the mask and spilled some but greedily guzzled the rest. In replacing the mug beside the hot plate on the stand this time he never made it, nor did he mind, for he chuckled and watched the mug bounce across the cement floor toward the fireplace. Then he relaxed deliciously in the wheelchair with a sigh of pure voluptuous anticipation as behind him the transceiver's buzzer again sounded and again the red signal light below the zero-beat dial flashed on. Lars Johannsen moved not a muscle nor gave any sign he heard.

But Bucher head. And Kate Pernod heard. Though

not so much the buzzer now as Goober Howard speaking. Something was wrong! Bad wrong; Bucher felt it like the choke of death, something suddenly ghastly terribly wrong, his world disintegrating. Bucher sprang to the transceiver, to tune it, adjust it, to aid reception for Goober's words, hysterical words, hysterical cries of childlike condemnation, came across the distance in brief snatches only, sharply defined spurts, dashes of articulation. Abruptly Bucher knew the fault was Goober's, and therefore left the receiver-audio dial alone, hoping, straining, for the young giant to stop rotating the frequency-selector dial of his sister's set. This hope at last was realized. They heard the voice of Goober Howard with greater clarity but due to his hysteria still in snatches, not coherently.

". . . don't like . . . Bloody Foreground . . . you Mr. Bucher . . . and Granny . . . of say . . . you . . . Sissy-Glyss . . . you come here . . . that for nobody . . . awful Simon Sipes . . . ain't none . . . dying . . . then only . . ."

"Bucher, who is it?" Kate whispered from beside him.

"Goober Howard. And they're in trouble." He whirled toward the red door and the freight helicopter beyond, flinging back over his shoulder: "So long, Lars." But Lars Johannsen did not hear, would never hear again.

Ludicrous in cotton-print housedress with the Super-Hot submachine gun strapped across her back, Kate Pernod scrambled into the copilot seat of the dead Kroger's helicopter as from the cockpit Bucher activated the remote-control power unit, sliding back the hangar section of the roof. Desperate urgency thrust aside his caution and the freighter leaped skyward through the opening above with motor insufficiently warm. At two hundred feet an unseen force struck from above and a high-tension scream wrenched free of Kate's lips while the craft plunged toward earth. Bucher threw the power feed wide open, held it wide open, cursing in vicious bursts and the craft coughed, shuddered, and ceased to plunge when its prop-blades bit the air, caught, held, chewed the air savagely and swept the ship across the first summit

177

in the direction of the Howards' place with inches to spare, rocketing across the ridges until it dived to within twenty feet of the earth in the valley above their destination, and Kate clenched her eyes against the sight of the Howard stone house and barn hurtling at them with sickening speed and shook as one seized by a violent ague. She did not recall landing, only a bone-jarring jolt, then Bucher racing for the rear of the house and the screened porch where a young Hercules wept and wrung his hands in despair.

"What's wrong, Goob? Tell me!"

And when the boy told him the color drained from Bucher's face to leave the mottled pasty hue of aged dough, and he plunged on across the porch, into the house, down the book-lined hall to the bedroom in silence sobbing:

"Please God have mercy!" the first prayer of his life.

Then he was with her, beside her, seated on the edge of the bed where lay his dear-lovely sweet-lovely soft-lovely rare-lovely entrancing and fascinating dainty mountain nymph. And his soul was sick unto death inside him.

"Why!?" The voice he did not know as his, the sound of it was strange to him. "In God's holy name—*why!?*" Beside the head of the bed was a nightstand and in the agony of his grief he lashed out with a balled fist to vent a part of his stifling despair on the object of his hate. But it was only the cup, an empty cup, the deadly brew it held before no longer there. The cup shattered against the wall, the pieces scattering about the floor.

"In God's name, Pepper, *why?*"

"I no longer want to live. I cannot live and bear the burden of my guilt, not even for you, my darling Badman."

Her voice was scarcely audible, faint, without life, and he was forced to strain to hear, but benumbed by anguish and not understanding, he said nothing in return.

"I was told of what you did at Boogerville, Sir Badman. You talked with Lars Johannsen? Yes, I know. I

178

talked to him also, by radio. Poor Lars. So trusting and so kind. Did he tell you how we got the laboratory operation started. His lab and all? He'll never know it did not happen as he thinks, could not happen as he thinks it did. There was no money.

"I meant to tell you he was my one-day husband, and would have—I had no thought to deceive you, Sir Badman. Though now it doesn't matter.

"The money left to Goob and me, by Lars, all but a little, was spent in keeping him alive. When he went to Ohio and Goob and I came back here to live I had only a few thousand left—which I spent on fixing this place up. After this I got in touch with Q-Boy Kroger and told him of my plan, which he bought and which he sold to the Syndicate. No one but Kroger ever knew of my true connection with the place. I stayed away from the lab and from anything that even remotely smacked of the lab. Kroger ran the place—that was part of our bargain. The moonshine still was my cover. And that's it. You know the rest—except that I have the innocent blood of thirteen people on my wretched soul—the Tiptons? And now you know that too. I'd always thought the Rudds guilty of that fiendish atrocity until today, when Simon Sipes drove around by the highway from Boogerville and told me the truth. It was really I who killed them because it was I who brought Q-Boy Kroger and his hideous pack of monsters into these mountains. Therefore the guilt is mine. The Tiptons' blood is on my head. And soon now I shall commence to pay for it throughout eternity.

"Zubrio's little black notebook that you wanted, and the two million dollars Lars also sent, are on that chest of drawers across the room. And do not worry over Goober's welfare, nor Granny's, for they are well taken care of and have been for a long time. Dolly Fancher knows what to do and will see to it that it gets done."

At last Bucher found his voice and was about to speak, but noticed Pepper's mouth moving yet heard nothing. Her voice was too weak; she was too far gone. Bucher fought mightily with himself not to scream and tear at his hair, and won, then leaned over and placed an ear against her lips—

"Will you do something for me, Sir Badman? Not today, nor tomorrow, nor even soon, but sometime when you want to and only if you want to; but go alone, go there all by yourself, and sit a while and think of me, and you, remembering how we were and how it was with us at our Secret Place."

An eternity of sixty seconds ticked past before Bucher straightened, again choked with emotion that sought to hamper speech, but this time he would not permit it, and swiftly ran through his mind the words of his promise to return to their Secret Place, then forced himself to smile. But said nothing. There was no use. Pepper would not have heard him.

Nor did Bucher hear himself, at least he retained no memory of the harsh, raw sounds that told of a strong man's grief as he sat there on the edge of the bed where the dead girl lay, one of her fragile, delicate hands in both of his as he patted it lightly from time to time. Later, though how much later Bucher was never to know, he folded her arms in rest and, for a moment longer, before he drew the sheet from the chest of drawers over her completely, stood there seeing her with a pert little smile on her lips and remembering how she laughed. After this he covered her with the sheet and turned toward the door, a weary slump in his big shoulders and the bitter-sour taste of defeat in his mouth.

THE "BUTCHER,"
the only man to leave
the Mafia—and live!
A man forever on the run,
unable to trust anyone,
condemned to a life
of constant violence!

THE BUTCHER SERIES

Order		Title	Book #	Price
_____	# 1	KILL QUICK OR DIE	P011	$ .95
_____	# 2	COME WATCH HIM DIE	P025	$ .95
_____	# 3	KEEPERS OF DEATH	P084	$ .95
_____	# 4	BLOOD DEBT	P111	$ .95
_____	# 5	DEADLY DEAL	P152	$ .95
_____	# 6	KILL TIME	P197	$ .95
_____	# 7	DEATH RACE	P228	$ .95
_____	# 8	FIRE BOMB	P272	$ .95
_____	# 9	SEALED WITH BLOOD	P279	$ .95
_____	#10	THE DEADLY DOCTOR	P291	$ .95
_____	#11	VALLEY OF DEATH	P332	$ .95
_____	#12	KILLER'S CARGO	P429	$1.25
_____	#13	BLOOD VENGEANCE	P539	$1.25
_____	#14	AFRICAN CONTRACT	P583	$1.25

AND MORE TO COME . . .

TO ORDER

Please check the space next to the book/s you want, send this order form together with your check or money order, include the price of the book/s and 25¢ for handling and mailing to:

PINNACLE BOOKS, INC. / P.O. Box 4347
Grand Central Station / New York, N.Y. 10017

☐ **CHECK HERE IF YOU WANT A FREE CATALOG**

I have enclosed $_____ check_____ or money order_____
as payment in full. No C.O.D.'s

Name_____

Address_____

City_____ State_____ Zip_____
(Please allow time for delivery)

the Executioner

PINNACLE BOOKS

The gutsiest, most exciting hero in years.
Imagine a guy at war with the Godfather
and all his Mafioso relatives! He's rough,
he's deadly, he's a law unto himself —
nothing and nobody stops him!

THE EXECUTIONER SERIES by DON PENDLETON

Order		Title	Book#	Price
_____	# 1	WAR AGAINST THE MAFIA	P401	$1.25
_____	# 2	DEATH SQUAD	P402	$1.25
_____	# 3	BATTLE MASK	P403	$1.25
_____	# 4	MIAMI MASSACRE	P404	$1.25
_____	# 5	CONTINENTAL CONTRACT	P405	$1.25
_____	# 6	ASSAULT ON SOHO	P406	$1.25
_____	# 7	NIGHTMARE IN NEW YORK	P407	$1.25
_____	# 8	CHICAGO WIPEOUT	P408	$1.25
_____	# 9	VEGAS VENDETTA	P409	$1.25
_____	#10	CARIBBEAN KILL	P410	$1.25
_____	#11	CALIFORNIA HIT	P411	$1.25
_____	#12	BOSTON BLITZ	P412	$1.25
_____	#13	WASHINGTON I.O.U.	P413	$1.25
_____	#14	SAN DIEGO SIEGE	P414	$1.25
_____	#15	PANIC IN PHILLY	P415	$1.25
_____	#16	SICILIAN SLAUGHTER	P416	$1.25
_____	#17	JERSEY GUNS	P417	$1.25
_____	#18	TEXAS STORM	P418	$1.25
_____	#19	DETROIT DEATHWATCH	P419	$1.25
_____	#20	NEW ORLEANS KNOCKOUT	P475	$1.25
_____	#21	FIREBASE SEATTLE	P499	$1.25
_____	#22	HAWAIIAN HELLGROUND	P625	$1.25

AND MORE TO COME . . .

TO ORDER

Please check the space next to the book/s you want, send this order
form together with your check or money order, include the price of
the book/s and 25¢ for handling and mailing to:

PINNACLE BOOKS, INC. / P.O. Box 4347
Grand Central Station / New York, N.Y. 10017

☐ CHECK HERE IF YOU WANT A FREE CATALOG

I have enclosed $_____ check_____ or money order_____
as payment in full. No C.O.D.'s

Name_____

Address_____

City_____ State_____ Zip_____
(Please allow time for delivery)

THE RAZONI & JACKSON SERIES

One's black, one's white—they're young and the ballsiest detectives on the city beat! Dynamite—and exclusively from Pinnacle!

by W. B. MURPHY

Order	Book No.	Title	Price
_____	P163-2	CITY IN HEAT, #1	.95
_____	P194-7	DEAD END STREET, #2	.95
_____	P267-1	ONE NIGHT STAND, #3	.95
_____	P363-3	DOWN & DIRTY, #4	.95
_____	P426-1	LYNCH TOWN, #5	$1.25

and more to come . . .
